FINDING FINN

WOLF'S MATE MPREG ROMANCE

KIKI BURRELLI

Finding Finn: Wolf's Mate Mpreg Romance

Proofreading by Jennifer Smith, LesCourt Author Services

Formatting by Leslie Copeland, LesCourt Author Services

CONNECT WITH KIKI

Join my newsletter!

And stay up to date on my newest titles, giveaways, and news!

Join the Pack! Awooooo!

Come hang out with your pack mates!

Visit Kiki's Den on Facebook and join the pack! Enjoy exclusive access to behind the scenes excerpts, cover reveals and surprise giveaways!

EXPERIENCE THE WOLF'S MATE WORLD

Finding Finn

Claiming Christian

Saving Sorell

Protecting Pippen

Fighting for Frannie (MMF)

To AB

;) For helping me with research.

CHAPTER ONE

"You have your toiletries bag?" Finn's mother asked him yet again. She'd asked variations of the same question from the moment she'd picked him up from Cedar Hills Behavioral Health Institute. He'd assumed having to pick up your twenty-five-year-old son after he had been committed for four months for attempting suicide would make a mother worried and forgetful.

"Yes, Mom. Besides, I'm sure Frannie will lend me some toothpaste or toilet paper if I forgot them."

Finn's mom pursed her lips. Her cherry red lipstick had worn to the lip line. She wasn't happy that Finn had all but demanded to stay with his younger sister during family therapy sessions. In fact, Finn had gone as far as to make it a condition of his own release. He had no intentions of hurting his mother, but knew even a week under her well-meaning care would slap him right back to where he'd just been released. Probably not for the same reason. Hopefully.

That had all been an accident. Finn brushed the puckered scar at his wrist. Yeah, he'd cut his wrist and okay, he didn't immediately try to apply pressure or find a band-aid, but it hadn't been for the reason everyone thought. The blood leaking from his body had been so surreal, beautiful in its finality. Try explaining that to a roommate who already looked at you like a bomb about to go off. Finn's roommate had gone straight to the university apartment security station, and the rest was history.

Finn didn't judge him too harshly. It had probably been scary for his roommate, stumbling across Finn in his boxers, standing in the kitchenette, a knife in his hand, staring at the blood coating his arm.

Finn sat back in the passenger seat of his mom's Oldsmobile. He enjoyed the summer sun flashing across his face. He didn't think he still belonged in the institute but, he had issues, never felt like he belonged. Even during family photos, Finn would offer to be the one taking the picture. He'd failed at any team sport, despite his naturally athletic build.

His mom pulled off the highway, taking a maple tree-lined exit that would bring them to Frannie's neighborhood. Finn had always struggled in finding where he fit, his purpose. But, he'd learned in therapy that *everyone* struggled with that. And if they didn't, then they were lying.

He was re-energized by this new revelation and had all the motivation he needed to get his life back on track. He'd been forced to drop out of his graduate studies in clinical psychology when he'd been committed, but he hadn't really missed that much of the curriculum. A couple weeks of studying hard and a handful of aptitude tests should be all he needed to get back in the program. The university might need to do a few psychological evaluations. Finn might have to ask the instructors who'd given him letters of recommendation the first time around to do so again, but he was confident he would get back in and set his life back on track. Easy as that.

It *wouldn't* be *easy as that* though if Finn had his mother hovering over his shoulder every second of the day asking how he was feeling and if he was hungry and, did he take his meds? Besides, of all of his five family members, Finn was most comfortable with Frannie. His mother hovered, his dad was perpetually irritated by him, and his older brothers, Felix and Farley alternated between torturing him or ignoring him. Francesca—Frannie—mostly left him alone. She didn't ignore him but didn't pester him with a lot of questions or demands. She just let him...breathe.

Finn's mom stopped at the curb in front of Frannie's modest but stylish one-story home. The building itself looked more like a cottage, but the neighborhood was stellar. Food carts on the corner fostered an excellent nightlife, plus, it was close to the university that Finn had been attending before. He brushed his scar again, the motion was becoming something of a security blanket for him. He stopped though when he looked over at his mother and saw her eyes widen with shock.

"Mom." Finn faked a smile and tried to sound calm. "It is going to be fine. Alright? I'm better now." He hauled his duffel higher up his arm and opened the door. "Thank you for the ride. I'll call you later."

She grabbed his arm. "Maybe I should help you get settled? I don't see Frannie's car. Have you even tried using that phone yet? You bought it at the gas station for goodness' sake."

This time, he really did smile. "Frannie has a phone too. I don't think she bought hers at a gas station." He swung a leg out and stepped onto the pavement, but his mom didn't let go.

"Finn. I...just. I don't know what I would do if..." Her eyes filled with tears and Finn had to look away. He caught his own image in the side mirror, dirty blond hair, boring brown eyes. How much of a shitbag was he that he made his mother worry so much? A rising tide of hatred welled up inside of him. He didn't deserve such a loving, caring mom. She'd be better off not having to worry anymore.

Sensing more dark thoughts, Finn closed his eyes and forced himself to silently repeat the mantra he'd been taught during group therapy.

I am worthy. I am worthy. I am worthy.

When he opened his eyes, he avoided the side mirror. Instead, he leaned back into the car and pulled his mom into a hug. "You won't have to know, Mom. I promise. I swear. You should go now, it's Tuesday. You get your nails done on Tuesdays," he said like he was trying to prove how normal he was. "Maybe we can have lunch later this week. Thursday?" He spoke while still hugging her. Her darker, curly hair tickled his cheek.

She sniffled and nodded. Finn managed to step all the way out of the car this time and shut the door. True to her nature, his mom waited for Finn to fish the second key out from under a ceramic alligator in a tutu near the front door and open the door before she drove off.

Finn shut the door behind himself, leaned with his back against it and breathed in a calming breath. It was dark inside Frannie's house and cold.

"Frannie? Francesca?" he called out, thinking now how strange it really was that she hadn't at least come out to say hi to their mom. The front door and entryway led directly to a wide living room with windows at the front and a wall at the back that acted as part of the hallway. There was a brown sectional couch in an L shape around a wicker coffee table and a large plasma television that hung on the wall. He wondered how she'd gotten that installed but figured she'd probably had the delivery guy do it. Frannie was great at getting guys to do what she wanted.

He stepped through the living room to the kitchen. Straight ahead was the marble-topped island and on the other side sat the fridge, sink, and window that looked out onto her patio and yard. The appliances were all either marbled or stainless, and she had a gas stove and oven. It was really a great house. Frannie had started raking it in writing romance books online. Finn didn't know if his parents knew that yet or if they still thought she was a free-lance editor.

Finn plopped his duffel on the island. There was a note there being held down by a can of light beer. He recognized Frannie's impatient scribble.

Welcome home, Randle! How was the cuckoo's nest? Joking, joking. Anyway, I'm not home. You can probably tell by now. But, don't worry, I will text mom and tell her you settled in beautifully. Enjoy this, most likely warm by now, beer.

Finn smiled. This was why Frannie was his favorite. Somehow, she had known he would need some alone time to settle. Get his shit back together. Her note continued:

I'll be back by Saturday most likely. Early next week at the latest, probably. Oh and don't freak out, but—

Just then, there was a distinct sound of someone moving behind him. Someone who was trying to be very quiet. Frannie didn't have a live-in boyfriend or a girlfriend. This was a friendly neighborhood, but nice neighborhoods attracted robbers, right? Finn tensed. He heard one more clear, heavy, ominous step and snatched the can of light beer, spun, and hurtled it toward the sound.

The can met its mark, hitting a huge man right in the forehead before bouncing off and clanging to the floor. It didn't knock him over or even stall him much. Finn caught a glimpse of the man's dark hair and blue eyes before launching himself on top of the intruder, trying to knock him down.

He'd literally leaped on the man, but the intruder still didn't fall. Instead, he'd managed to catch Finn and restrain him by holding him tightly to his chest, pinning both of his arms between them. Finn struggled, not a small man by most standards. He was considered fit, but this guy managed to catch and hold on to him like he was a child.

"Let me go, fucker! My sister is going to be home any minute!" Finn lied.

The man with the chiseled jaw didn't speak, and he didn't set him down either.

Finn changed tactics. "I just got out of the crazy hospital. Do you want me to go insane on you?"

That got a smile from his stoic face. Oddly, Finn noticed he had dimples when he smiled.

Why the hell do you care if this asshole has dimples? Finn opened his mouth again, gearing up to say something genuinely scathing, something that was sure to scare the big man off.

The big man noticed Finn's parted lips and scowled. He set Finn down, slowly, to his feet. "Your sister, Frannie, she left a note," he said with a voice as smooth as forty-year-old scotch. "She was supposed to warn you I would be here."

Finn exhaled loudly, only noticing then that he'd been holding his breath. He felt a pang in his gut when the guy had said Frannie's name. He must be a new boyfriend. With his broad shoulders and huge biceps, he looked like he could be her type. Hell, he looked like *anyone's* type.

Finn physically shook the train of thought from his head. His sexual preferences were confusing and not really important to him until this point. As unimportant as it had been, he'd still never thought of himself as gay. So then why did he feel a tiny bit sad when he discovered this guy was here for Frannie? *The institution warped you, buddy. Does it to the best of us.*

Finn backed up, away from the man, careful to never turn away. He bumped into the island, reached blindly for the note and brought it around so he could see the guy and read at the same time.

Oh, and don't freak out, but my buddy Luke needed a place to stay for a couple weeks too. There's more than enough room, so I figured, the more, the merrier. Don't worry, Luke just looks big and scary, he is really a puppy dog. Have a great time!-Frannie

P.S. I locked up all the kitchen knives.

P.P.S. Joke, no I didn't, but DON'T YOU DARE MAKE ME WISH I HAD!

Finn blushed furiously reading the last line of her note.

"Everything okay?" the man, Luke, asked. He rubbed at a red spot on his forehead. Finn noticed a small bump already forming.

"Shit, fuck, dude, I am sorry." Finn grabbed a towel and pushed the button on the fridge for the ice dispenser. He wrapped a couple of cubes up and stretched his arm out, almost like he was going to put the ice up against Luke's forehead himself. At the last minute, he caught himself and handed the towel to the guy instead.

"Thanks," Luke mumbled. "You have a pretty strong right arm. Play any baseball?"

"I played little league in grade school, but got kicked off the team for apologizing too much."

Luke looked like he was going to laugh. "What were you apologizing for?"

"For being there." The moment he said it, he wondered why. What was it about this guy that made him want to throw out something so personal? Most likely, Finn's subconscious wanted to scare Luke away nice and early so that Finn wouldn't have to worry about Luke wanting to hang out or do anything together. He had shit to do, tests to study for, a life to get back to. He didn't have time to hit the bars or play wingman or whatever it was guys did.

That was, if he wasn't already dating Frannie. Even if he wasn't, Finn didn't think a guy like Luke would need a wingman. Not with his piercing stare, square jaw and broad, muscular chest...

What the actual fuck, Finn? He turned all the way around, not caring that his back was to him. His body was acting strangely. Again, he blamed his time at the institute. This was what four months of self-discovery would do to a person. He opened the fridge and snagged the rest of the six-pack of light beer.

Luke eyed the five-pack in his hand. Finn yanked one out of the plastic rings and handed it to Luke while being very careful that their fingers did not touch. Then, he hauled his duffel back up and with a short wave over his shoulder, headed down the hallway to the guest bedroom he usually stayed in. As he stepped through the doorway, he heard Luke crack open the can.

"Nice to meet you," Luke called a moment before Finn shut the door.

He tossed the duffel on the bed and leaned against the cool wood. His body felt like he'd just sprinted a mile, skin flushed, heart beating wildly. He was sure if he swiped a finger over his forehead that it would come off sweaty. Was there something wrong with him? An adverse reaction to his meds?

He had no prejudice toward anyone's sexual preference. It was more that he'd always felt separate from the crushing and lusting that had gone on around him. He'd never been interested much in...anyone.

What was he even going on about now? He wasn't interested in Luke, he was his sister's boyfriend for goodness' sake. It had to be the adrenaline coursing through his body when he'd thought he was a robber. There were documented studies of people developing feelings they wouldn't normally during times of duress.

Finn chuckled once, nervously. It felt nice to have a logical excuse for whatever it was that raced through him. Now he could work on forgetting it.

CHAPTER TWO

Luke's feet got wet in the growing pool of light beer spreading across the hardwood floor. The thin aluminum casing of the beer can in his hand had been no match for his claws. Usually—no not usually—always, Luke *always* had control over his animal instincts. He couldn't say that anymore, not with the proof of his uninhibited moment covering more and more of the hardwood floor.

A small mess and a destroyed can were acceptable casualties to Luke. The interaction between him and Finn could be considered nothing but a success. Especially if he took into account what he had really wanted to do the moment he'd left the guest room and spotted his friend's brother. With a lean soccer player's body, and a round ass like a dream, Finn had bent over the kitchen island, practically offering himself to Luke.

Luke had immediately gone into full animal stalk mode. No wonder Finn had been terrified at first. People didn't enjoy being hunted, and that was precisely what he had been doing. He'd crept as close as he could with the intent of claiming, mounting.

Luckily, Finn had thrown that first beer can at him. Luke's tunnel vision level of focus had been the only reason his reflexes hadn't been fast enough to catch the flying can in the first place. It had knocked a little sense into him, and just as the lust-filled haze had begun to clear, Finn had jumped on him.

Luke tried to sit on the stool at the island, but his dick had other ideas, jutting and straining out so tightly against his jeans that it was uncomfortable to bend that way. So, he grabbed a mop instead and replayed the moment over and over in his mind. His inner wolf had immediately begun tracking Finn, noticing each movement as if he had been moving in slow motion. Then, Finn had done the unexpected, went on the offensive and leaped. Luke had wrapped his arms around him absolutely sure that all was lost to his instincts. He'd been milliseconds from throwing Finn on the floor, tearing his clothes off his body and mounting him. Except then Finn had started on about being a crazy maniac, and he'd been able to let go. Not that it had been easy.

Even now, with the length of a hallway and a closed door separating them, Luke found it difficult not to break down the flimsy wood and claim the man as his mate. And there was his second problem. Wolf shifters took mates, that wasn't unusual. But Luke was gay, had known since his teens. He was in his thirties now and always assumed that his sexual preference was what kept him from finding that one person in the world he was meant to be with. There had been others that he'd found, more than he really liked to think about, but they had been mutual beneficial relationships.

He'd assumed that the wolf inside most shifters demanded a mate to breed, and you couldn't breed with another man, so that had meant to Luke that he was exempt from the whole mating process. One glance at his fingertips, where claws were still distended instead of fingernails and at his raging hard-on that squeezed so firmly against his jeans he was sure he'd be able to read the cleaning instructions off of his cock and Luke began to think he was not exempt.

Not only was he not exempt but his mate was now staying in the same house he was, one short hallway away.

What had Frannie said before she left for that retreat? Don't worry, you won't even notice he's here. Finn is so unassuming I thought I only had two brothers for the first five years of my life.

Unassuming? Alluring, feisty and seductive maybe. How could anyone not notice him? Luke definitely couldn't.

Now, he came to the last, most devastating issue. Finn hadn't seemed anywhere near as affected by him. Here he was, pacing the kitchen with a mop in his hand like a lazy dance partner while the only man to ever make Luke lose his cool sat in another room, decidedly cold.

He growled in frustration. Then froze and eyed Finn's bedroom door to see if he'd growled too loudly. Frannie knew about his shifter tendencies. He'd agreed to be interviewed by her as research for her books. But, the average, normal person didn't know about wolf shifters or shifters in general and the average person was happy that way.

If Luke stood in that kitchen any longer, Finn would have first-hand experience when it came to wolf shifters and what wolf shifters did when they found their mate. And then, not only would his good friend Frannie hate him, but Luke would hate himself. Just thinking about losing his control enough that he caused harm to Finn made a knot grow in his stomach. No. He was a monster, but not that type of monster.

A short chuckle came from Finn's room. What was he laughing at? Already, Finn had moved on from their brief, explosive interaction. The sound agitated Luke's ears, made his heart beat faster and his dick even harder. Like sex-filled nails on a lusty chalkboard.

Part of his ordinarily excellent control relied on Luke knowing his limits and right now, they were reached. Luke didn't bother walking back to his room for a change. Sure, he had beer all over his pants, but he didn't know if he would be strong enough to walk past Finn's bedroom twice. Thankfully, he had his wallet already in his pocket. After wiping the floor once more, he stowed the mop back in the closet and left out the front door.

The day had been hot and although it was dusk, it was still warm and the middle of summer so the streets were busy. Luke had spent so much of his adult life as a lone wolf, crowds and urban areas grated at him. He didn't mind it so much inside of Frannie's house but walking alone, he felt twitchy and paranoid. Up ahead on the corner was the 45th Corner Pub, the closest thing he had to a regular joint. They had cheap beers and even cheaper shots of whiskey.

"Hey, Luke," the waitress, Christina, said with a wink. She'd found out she was barking up the wrong tree his first night in with Frannie, but unlike other girls, she didn't seem to mind and still flirted endlessly.

He gave her a wave and walked straight to the bar, taking a seat at the wooden, high-backed barstool.

"How come you never sit in my section anymore?" That was Christina again, sidling up to him, swinging her hips so hard Luke thought they might snap.

"This place isn't that big. The whole thing is your section."

She pretended to think on that while tapping a manicured finger against her lips. Luke had no doubt that move of hers had her other male patrons sweating all over. "True, except for the one place you always seem to want to sit, at the bar. Are you still mad at me? C'mon, baby, I already promised never to try to set you up again."

Luke ignored her and ordered a shot and a pint from the owner who worked behind the bar. He was an older no-nonsense type. He'd clearly lived a life, saw some shit. Luke had never heard him utter a single word all the times he'd come. He liked him.

Luke downed the shot and quickly signaled for another. The second went down as smooth as the first, and soon, he ordered his third. This would be a quick night.

"I thought you bear types liked the barely legal—"

"I am not a bear," Luke growled.

Christina shuddered lasciviously and rubbed the sides of her body in an overtly sexual way. "I love it when you get angry."

Luke smirked. She was likable, if not a little annoying. "Don't you have other customers?" he prompted with no anger behind his words. He could handle a sassy waitress. What he really wanted to handle was a heartbreakingly solemn man with a mean throw.

"Are you gonna listen to the man or do you want to hump his leg first?" a grisly voice asked from behind Luke.

Instantly, Luke's hackles rose, and the hairs on the back of his neck stood straight up. It must have been the whiskey that had kept Luke from sensing the other shifter the second he'd stepped in.

Christina shifted from sass to something harder. "Excuse me—"

"No, Christina, I'll handle it. Besides, your other customers do look thirsty."

She must have seen something in his face because the spunky waitress retreated without a snarky comment.

"Imagine my surprise," the other man continued, sitting down on the barstool beside him and sliding Luke's untouched pint in front of himself, "when I heard that there was a lone wolf in this territory. A lone wolf? Here? Well, I thought it best to find this young pup and lead him in the right direction." He downed the contents of the pint in a few large gulps. "Now, imagine my even larger fucking surprise when I discover this lone wolf isn't just some lost nobody, but the wannabe alpha, booted from his pack as a wee faggy pup." He reached across Luke, grabbed the shot glass and downed the contents. "Your pa says hello, by the way."

For once, Luke's animal and Luke the person were in total agreement. He whipped his arm out and cupped the other man at the back of his head, slamming his face forward against the edge of the bar. The guy groaned and slid to the floor. Blood spurted from his nose. "No, he doesn't," Luke said calmly, evenly, standing over the groaning form. "My father hasn't spoken to me since I was sixteen. Get the fuck out of here and don't come back."

"Luke?" Christina shrieked with no small amount of fear.

"I'm sorry, babe." He pulled out a hundred dollar bill and tossed it on the counter. "You should probably call the cops before this dickwad finds his feet."

He had to force his legs to calm down, to keep his pace even on the sidewalk. He wasn't scared, far from it. Luke felt alive. His inner wolf howled its approval and Luke felt like howling right along with it. That had been better than a shot of top-shelf whiskey, better than a pay per view game you didn't have to pay for, better than sex...

He stopped in his tracks.

It might have been better than normal sex, but it sure as hell couldn't hold a candle against the sex he would never have with his mate if he ended up dead because Luke couldn't keep his goddamn temper.

Luke did run now, the few blocks down and over, back to the house that was covered with his scent. He slammed the door open. "Finn!" he bellowed. "Finn, grab your shit, we need to—"

Finn came around the corner of the hallway wearing a tight white v-neck t-shirt and plaid boxers that clung to his thighs and did nothing to hide his erection. He groggily scratched the back of his head, mussing his dirty blond hair while looking up under his lashes at Luke with the sexiest come-fuck-me stare. "What the hell man?" he said with a yawn. Luke smelled the beer on him. Had he slammed the rest of that six-pack?

"Pack your bags," Luke said with more anger than he'd intended.

Heartbreak, anger, sadness and then bleak acceptance was what he saw on Finn's face, in that order. "Did Frannie change her mind? She couldn't kick me out herself, so she sent her boyfriend?"

"Boyfriend?"

"Man-thing, friend with benefits, fuck-buddy, whatever. I don't need to know the gruesome terms of your relationship. The end result is the same. Tell her thanks for letting me take a nap here."

Luke was often silent but not because he was at a loss

for words. He searched his brain for the right words now but found only growls. "I'm—I'm not sleeping with your sister. She isn't the sibling I—it doesn't matter. My point is, I'm not fucking Frannie." Somehow, he managed to stutter through what he wanted to say.

A moment of silence and then, "Okay."

Okay? "Finn, we have to go, both of us. I'll get the word out to Frannie, but—"

"I'm not going anywhere with you," Finn said, turning from him, *dismissing* him.

Oh no. That would not do. Luke vaulted in front of him, standing in his face, his space. "I'm trying to keep you safe."

"From what? The most dangerous thing I can see is you. You smell like liquor and look like you ran here. You don't know anything about me so just leave me alone so I can get back to bed. I was having this really great dream about—"

He stopped talking abruptly. Suspiciously abrupt.

It could've been his wolf's vision, or maybe anyone would've noticed the way Finn blushed and then the way his deep brown eyes fell down to Luke's lips, as if the motion was involuntary, the way his tongue licked his own lips as he did.

A growl ripped from Luke's throat that was all wolf. He crushed his lips against the other man's, claiming his mouth. For one heart-stopping moment, Finn was stiff as a tree against him, but then he sighed into Luke's mouth, all at once giving as good as he was taking.

Luke already knew what it felt like to hold Finn and he needed that feeling again. He lifted Finn up, a wide palm on each ass cheek. Finn immediately wrapped his legs around Luke's waist, anchoring himself against Luke's erection. He groaned, loving the friction and ripped his mouth away to kiss Finn's neck. Kisses turned into little nips that left red marks on his skin. He swelled with pride at the sight of the reddened skin. Luke had done that, and when anyone else saw the marks on Finn's skin, they would know he was taken and cared for. He licked over the spots he'd nibbled, loving the squeaking noises coming from Finn.

"Are you alright?" That was Luke the man asking. His inner wolf snarled at the prospect of giving his mate the smallest chance of refusing them, refusing this.

"Shut the fuck up," Finn replied in a human version of a snarl. The wolf approved. He bucked forward, unexpectedly, thrusting his erection against Luke's. He pitched back, falling off balance and they landed on one side of the sectional sofa, tumbling over the top and back on the floor.

Finn was on fire. His skin was flushed, his dick rock hard. He'd been a little buzzed when he went to sleep and woke up from a dream where he had been, well doing precisely the same thing he was doing now, except in the dream, he had fewer clothes on.

Straight, gay, bi...he didn't know what he was now. He didn't care. All he knew was that he needed to get his boxers off. He needed to feel Luke's cock, now. But the imposing man was suddenly treating him with kid gloves, rubbing his arms up and down and then letting his hands graze along the curve of Finn's ass. They'd landed on the living room floor, may have already broken the coffee table. Finn would replace it. A small price.

He twisted around, the other man loomed powerfully over him. He grabbed for the buttons at Luke's jeans. Luke made a strangled noise and helped him pull his pants down and over his ass. Finn licked his lips at the sight of the cock that sprang out and into his face. Long—longer than his—and thick. It felt like the most natural thing in the world to wrap his lips around it and let his mouth slide down, down the shaft until he felt the head of him brush against the back of his throat.

Finn choked on it, but even that, he liked. Luke made a sound so raw it didn't seem human. Finn slid his mouth back out and then down again, a bit of fluid leaked into his mouth, and he was surprised to discover it actually tasted good. Sweeter than he'd been expecting and spicy. He moaned his pleasure at the taste, and that seemed Luke's undoing. He held Finn's face with a hand on either side of his head and fucked his mouth, shoving his cock into his inexperienced hole until he gagged. He let it slide nearly all the way out, just to push it back in again, keeping a relentless pace that made Finn's eyes water from the repeated use.

Finn loved every second of the carnal act. Never had he felt so full or complete. He let his wandering hand slide up Luke's leg until he found his balls, tight and constricted against a tense body. He brushed the sack with his fingers.

Luke howled. "I'm going to cum. Finn, are you ready?" His own name had never sounded sexier.

In response, he kept his lips tightly wrapped around Luke's dick. Finn brushed his sack more firmly and was rewarded by jet after jet of hot fluid. Abstractly, Finn had been ready for the man to cum, but he hadn't expected the force of it, and at first, some fell out of his mouth and dribbled down his chin. He was able to catch most of it though and swallowed it greedily, already addicted to the flavor of him.

"Turn over," Luke ordered as he was physically lifting

Finn and flipping him so that he was on his hands and knees on the carpet. "I need to taste you."

Finn thought if Luke needed to taste him then backside down would've been easier. Luke pulled his boxers down and using a hand on each cheek, spread Finn open so that his little pink hole was front and center. "There you are," Luke whispered reverently. His exhalation was a burst of hot air against the tight hole.

Finn was shocked into stillness. What did the man have planned? Would he like it?

Then, Luke licked a circle around the pucker, lapping at the skin there like it was an ice cream cone. Finn wailed, the sound full of lust and pleasure. Luke's tongue probing his hole was a feeling like no other, tingly and warm. It shoved tendrils of pleasure into each of his limbs, from his curling toes to his foggy, lust-filled head. Luke pushed his tongue into the hole, and Finn felt like he might pass out from the sensations. His head was light, and his breath came in gasps.

Luke reached around him and grabbed Finn's hard cock, giving it a good, firm, downward stroke. Immediately, a splash of precum coated Luke's fingers. He chuckled, and Finn felt the sound of it reverberate through his body.

"You were as turned on as I was earlier," Luke spoke to him through the haze. "You wanted this as much as me. Do you want to know why?"

Finn wanted his ass filled. He whimpered and angled his lower body upward in a silent invitation.

"Later then," Luke said though Finn wasn't sure he even knew what he'd been saying. Luke rose so that he was on his knees behind him and let the head of his cock rest against Finn's tight entrance.

Finn froze. Things like this required lube, or something

like that, right? He'd heard this sort of act could really hurt if both parties weren't prepared.

"Don't worry," Luke murmured. "This won't hurt, not how you are expecting." As he spoke, a jet of hot fluid dribbled out of his cock and against Finn's waiting hole. As it did, Finn felt the most amazing transformation. His asshole tingled like he'd applied a sensation-enhancing cream. Did the man have magic cum? It certainly felt that way as he was pushing the head of his cock in Finn's virgin hole and all Finn could feel was white-hot, blazing pleasure.

Soon, he was thankful for the magic cum. A handful of short thrusts and he felt full, although he knew Luke wasn't all the way in yet. He dared to look back over his shoulder and saw Luke's face of pure concentration. His shaft was only half buried in Finn's wanton ass.

"I can take it," he said through gritted teeth.

Luke grabbed his hips and groaned, pushing in an inch more "I don't want to hurt you."

"I want you to," Finn said, though, in truth, there wasn't anything unpleasant about it. More of just an overwhelming sense of fullness. He bucked back and was rewarded with a sharp hiss and more of Luke's cock. The heat of the man mounting him, the sounds of his steady breathing combined with Finn's own whimpers urged him into a possessed and needy state. "Come on, Luke, fuck me. This is my first time, so you have to make it good," he said between gasps.

The strong hands at his hips spasmed once in answer to Finn's confession. Then, Luke slid an arm under Finn's belly and slammed the rest of the way in. Finn felt Luke's balls slap against his own and he howled. Luke wasn't done, thrusting in and out with wild abandon as if he'd been taken over, consumed by something he had been trying too hard to hold back.

His other hand found Finn's cock and stroked it furiously as he thrust, brutally in and out. It didn't take Finn long to come all over the rug, and then Luke hunched over, his mouth at the crook where Finn's shoulder met his neck, and he bit down. Not enough to break the skin, but enough to keep him in place as Luke spilled the entire contents of his cock into Finn's no longer virgin asshole.

Finn couldn't have known what would happen next as Luke's cock seemed to swell even larger inside of him. It didn't hurt, like a distant part of his brain told him it should. Instead, the increased size nudged right up against his prostate. The feeling started slow and deep, like a nice massage, until almost immediately, Finn felt another orgasm rip violently through his body. It tore him apart, an endless rush of release that continued on and on until Finn couldn't keep his eyes open.

CHAPTER THREE

When Luke was finally able to separate himself from his animal side, he slid out of his mate. That that was the correct term for him was extremely clear to Luke now. Growing up and into his teen years, he remembered hearing whispers of lovers knotting inside their mates. He thought it was shifter legend. He knew better now.

Finn was definitely his mate.

Finn was also not conscious.

Luke crouched down, terrified he'd hurt him, gotten too rough. He remembered in the foggy front of his logical mind that Finn had said this was his first time. In fact, that had been the exact moment Luke had totally lost control.

He bent his head down to Finn's face. His light snore was a beautiful symphony to Luke's ears. Pride boiled inside of him, expanding so quickly he felt it would blast him apart. He'd fucked his mate senseless. He'd been *the first* man to fuck his mate senseless. That thought had his dick twitching and made the wolf in him begin to pace.

Oh no. *Finn needs sleep,* Luke told them both.

Luke thought back to the whole cause of this all. Time and physical exertion had cleared the liquor from his system and his amazing orgasm now allowed him to think logically.

There was no way that douche was alpha of this territory's pack. Luke still needed to be careful. That ass was no alpha, he wasn't a pack master, but was a pack mate, and Luke had no way of knowing how high up in the pack he was.

But, for right now, Luke had more important things to worry about. He noticed the room. Finn needed sleep and Luke needed to clean the place up. He stood, his foot landing on something that crunched. The wicker coffee table needed fixing.

Another crunch.

Or he needed to buy a new one.

He lifted Finn into his arms. The sleeping man snuggled up against his chest in the sexiest, sweetest way possible. Luke took him to Finn's room. He'd debated putting Finn in Luke's own bed, where he belonged, but ignored his wolf's demands and decided Finn waking up in a place that was at least a little bit familiar would be better. It would already be new for him to see Luke beside him when he woke.

He grabbed a towel from the bathroom, got it half wet with warm water and went back to Finn. Then he cleaned him up as best he could without disturbing him too much. Finn tossed a restless arm up and over his face so that it landed over his eyes, palm up.

Luke hissed at the jagged scar on his wrist. His wolf howled inside him. Who had dared hurt the man that was meant for him? Furious anger rose inside him. He studied the scar, committing it to memory, going through everything he already knew about Finn, all that Frannie had told him.

"I never knew where Finn was when I looked at him. He was always lost in his head. But I knew, wherever he was, he was torturing himself."

Luke gritted his teeth. He would have to address that behavior, but he could think of a hundred other conversations that should probably come before. Like, *hey I can turn into a wolf,* or *you are fated to be mine.* Yeah, there would be some other long talks that had to take precedence, but after, he would explain to Finn in no uncertain terms that he was too important to him—to the world—to try any shit like that again.

He tucked in Finn's naked body with a soft blanket he'd pulled from his own bed. The urge to smother him with his own scent was strong.

First on his to-do list was to clean up the living room, then he would go about fixing anything that could be fixed.

An hour or so later, Luke thought he'd done a convincing job erasing their spontaneous sexual encounter from Frannie's living room. The coffee table was toast though.

He looked at the clock. It was late, but if he was quick and took a cab, he should be able to buy a replacement coffee table and be back before Finn woke up. Above all else, Luke knew he needed to be by Finn's side when he opened his eyes.

Luke was gone and back in record time. He untied the heavy box from his motorcycle and hefted it up to the front door when he caught the familiar scent of a shifter. Not just another shifter. An old wolf shifter. Luke dropped the box and crouched, snarling in the direction of where the shifter stood. His canines grew long and sharp, making it the second time his alpha characteristics broke through his once strict hold on them.

An older man, with long salt and pepper hair and light blue eyes, stepped out of the darkness and into the light of the porch light. Standing where he was, the gray looked more like silver. His hands were raised in front of his body in surrender.

Luke compared him to his memory. The older shifter was still muscled but far less imposing. He also looked a lot older than Luke remembered. His hair had thinned and was a little longer, wilder than it had been. His face was more heavily lined, and his already pale eyes looked watery. Though, that could've been due to his penchant for shots of whiskey before breakfast.

"What are you doing here, old man?" Luke said, remaining in his protective crouch.

"That's a killer smile you've got, son," he replied, hands still up.

Luke took a hostile step toward the other man. At any other time, Luke might have backed away, disappeared into the background. He couldn't now that he had something precious to protect.

This couldn't be a coincidence. Luke hadn't seen this man for nearly twenty years, hadn't heard his voice for about ten. So then why had he tracked Luke down now of all times?

Luke didn't trust him, it had to have something to do with the guy at the bar. "I'm just here to talk, son. Clear things up."

"This isn't my house. I won't be asking you in," Luke said. He didn't trust his father—Daryl as he'd called him since the man had kicked him out—anywhere near Finn. But mostly, he didn't want the hate and anger the old man usually peddled to be anywhere near where it could affect Finn.

"There's a twenty-four-hour diner on the corner—"

"Yeah fucking right," Luke snapped. He wanted to curse. Why not just announce to the sly old man you have something inside the house to lose, dumbass?

If Daryl had caught on to the bit of information Luke hadn't meant to give, he didn't make any indication. He reached in his pocket slowly and pulled something small out. He tossed it toward Luke who caught it gingerly with one hand. In the center of his palm was a single canine tooth, long and curved, once sharp, now dull. His heartbeat quickened with the memory of a lost dream. Up until his sixteenth birthday, having one of these in his possession was all he had thought about. After, it had become a distant dream, too painful to remember clearly, more like something someone else had wanted that he'd heard about once.

Becoming a wolf shifter pack leader was not done by vote or popularity. It was earned through blood and often, if not always, it ended with the death of either the old pack leader or the contester. This tooth had belonged to whoever Luke's father's pack leader had killed to get the spot. Having it in his hand was the closest thing Luke would get to a promise that there was no trap in play.

"Lucian gives his word. He just wants you to hear me out."

"Why didn't your pack master come?"

"He didn't think this warranted a face to face. Lars is a good shifter, big mouth though."

Lars must've been that dick at the bar. "He was asking for a lot more than what he got."

"Still, we have things to discuss." He pointedly looked at the front door and back to Luke. "Grievances to air."

Luke wanted to tell him to fuck off. His wolf wanted to tell him to fuck off. But, he wasn't just thinking about himself anymore. If sitting down with the scum who had kicked him out onto the streets with no family just because he'd come out made his mate any safer, he'd do it. He had to.

"I know the place. It's close. I would know if anything was happening," he said.

"Fair enough."

LUKE SAT down in the empty diner with his face to the door. Tooth or not, he wasn't putting too much trust in the first man to really hurt him.

"Impressive display back there," Daryl said after a tired-looking waitress brought them two chipped mugs filled with black coffee. "Since when have your alpha traits been manifesting?"

"Is that what you came to talk to me about? My teeth?"

"No, I just thought all that shit had receded after...after," he waved his hand in front of his face in a vague motion.

"After you kicked me out, forced me away from and out of my pack and made me live alone in the wild? After you kept me from my family even after my own mother had died? After you told me she had died in a voicemail? After I was refused from every pack in the area on your order all because of my sexual preferences?"

"After you went lone," he said with a little of the steely tone Luke was more accustomed to.

"Is any of this important to what you came to say?" Luke didn't want to get into the exact cause of why his alpha characteristics were breaking through.

"So fucking stubborn. I am just trying to have a normal

conversation with my boy." His voice rose loud enough for the waitress to glance their way nervously.

"If you haven't noticed," Luke said with barely muted anger, "I am not your boy anymore. In fact, I am about the age you were when you sent me out to live 'lone' as you put it. So you will have to excuse the fuck out of me, actually no, I don't care if you excuse me or not. All I want is for you to say what you came to say, the message from your pack master and then go on your way." He worked hard to keep his tone level. It wouldn't do either of them any good if the waitress got spooked and called the cops.

"He says you can stay in the area—"

"How very generous."

His father leveled an icy stare in his direction. "You may have alpha blood in you, boy, but you don't have a pack to back you up. If you want to challenge, that is your prerogative, but until you do, you would have a better time if you showed my pack master some respect. Especially this pack master."

The alpha in him longed to do just as his father suggested. The urge was actually more powerful than he'd ever guessed it would be. Was it a part of gaining a mate? Wanting to be the most powerful in the territory? He wouldn't though, couldn't, not yet. "Fine. I can stay. Why especially this one? How is Lucian any different?"

Daryl leaned back, looking out the window and around the diner like he was suddenly worried someone was listening. "He's intense. A good, strong leader, but, you don't want to cross him."

That was fine with Luke. "I'm sensing there is a condition to my stay?"

"Just one. Don't mess with his pack again and don't

compete for resources. He has a tight hold on this area, and every pack surrounding is afraid of him. He'd like to keep it that way."

Luke didn't want a pack, he just wanted Finn. "That's it?"

"That's all I have for now."

He didn't miss the way his father avoided the actual question.

"You look different, son."

"I don't doubt that," Luke said sardonically.

"Boy, I will still put you over my knee and—"

Luke raised one eyebrow, and the old man had the decency to at least grin at the absurdity of what he'd said.

"Well, no, I guess I won't. But, come on, son. Do I have to rip out one of my own teeth and hand it to you to get you to talk? Not as pack representative, but as your father?"

Luke didn't want to talk to him about Finn. Not specifically. But he was curious about the mating process. First, he'd been too young to really understand what mating meant or how it had happened and then he'd spent the rest of his life thinking none of it applied to him. What was the old saying about wishing you'd paid attention in class?

"What do you know about mating?" Luke asked with a growl as if daring his dad to say anything derogatory.

"Why? Have you changed...I mean have you switched...or..."

"Never mind." Luke pushed the coffee mug from him so forcefully some of the liquid spilled over the lip and onto the table.

His dad actually reached across the table and grabbed his sleeve to keep him from standing and leaving. "No, I'm sorry. It's just that, well, I only know about one type of mating. And I really only know one thing about it. It is a tricky thing to find your mate. Done right and you can bet your ass your mate will be the best thing that ever happened to you."

"Done wrong?"

The old man flinched. "Hope you don't find out."

CHAPTER FOUR

WHEN FINN'S eyelids fluttered open, his hand immediately searched the space next to him on the bed as if by an instinct he hadn't known he possessed until that moment. It didn't matter though. The spot beside him was cold and empty.

He made a motion halfway between a yawn and a moan and stretched his arms above his head. His mouth felt dry, his body ached a little all over, but most importantly there was an altogether unfamiliar sore feeling at his backside. Then, he fully remembered the events of the night before. It had been...

Beautiful. Amazing. Hot.

If it was so beautiful and amazing then why was he in bed alone right now? Finn noticed he was clutching at the soft blanket he'd been wrapped in and threw it from his body. What did it mean that Luke wasn't here? What did the events mean to Finn and how he defined himself? He hadn't not enjoyed the events of the previous night. Though, he certainly didn't enjoy the feelings he had now.

Like he could tell he was coming down from an intense high and would soon grow cold from the inside out.

Finn leaped from bed, a sudden urgency to run from those feelings had him in the shower in seconds. The hot spray over his used body felt nice. He didn't linger though and was dressed and out the door, slowing down long enough to step around a big cardboard box on the front patio. On the front of the box was a picture of a dark wood coffee table.

So, Luke had gone and come back. He just hadn't bothered to stick around.

It wasn't until he was outside, zipping up his hoodie that Finn realized just how early it really was. The campus offices were long from being open. Even the library had a few hours. Though, Finn thought he'd relax just being nearer to campus. He already felt a bit keyed up, and the couple mile walk to the university would do him good.

There was a coffee shop on the edge of campus that opened early. There, Finn bought a black coffee and a plain bagel. He sat at a metal table outside the shop and pulled out his tablet.

Looking at the small rectangular device gave him a funny feeling. He hadn't used it since before his time at the institute. Electronics hadn't been allowed. It had been so long he nearly forgot his password. Soon though, the screen lit to life, and he was staring at his home screen. The background picture was the silhouette of a wolf, its head thrown back in mid-howl, muzzle pointed at the full moon.

His roommate had given him shit about the picture, saying it should be some 'hot chick' on a beach or something. Finn enjoyed this image though, it brought him a sense of calm whenever he felt the chaos that always threatened to inch closer. An image of some random girl on some random beach wouldn't do that for him.

Looking at the background image now, he didn't feel his normal calm. He felt peculiar. He took a sip of scalding coffee, swallowing the liquid and his feelings. His fingers found a familiar rhythm of tapping tabs and opening his email. His university email account had been deactivated after he'd left. His personal email inbox was full though. One bite into his bagel, and he saw most of the emails were shit. Ads for sales from stores he didn't remember ever shopping at. A few bills and statements. Luckily, he hadn't had a lot or owned very much before his time in treatment, so there weren't many bills for him to fall behind on. Who needed soul-crushing feelings of self-hate *and* a mountain of debt? Finn wanted to laugh at his own bitter joke. Instead, he closed his eyes and repeated his mantra.

I am worthy. I am worthy. I have a below average credit score but am also worthy.

He just needed to say it until he believed it.

Last night's crazy events flashed in his mind. He remembered Luke's growl just before he'd brushed his teeth against Finn's neck. Had Finn ever heard a sound as sexy as that? He gingerly touched the area on his neck. It was still a little sore. Was there a mark? He felt a stirring between his legs.

Calm down, buddy. Finn told himself. Well, he told that one part of himself. He had shit to do today. Shit that didn't include a too sexy nomadic stranger. Besides, where had that stranger been when Finn woke up? Not next to him. Not even in the same house by the sounds of it. He most definitely wasn't reminiscing wherever he was.

Finn brought his attention back to his inbox. One, toward the bottom of the page, caught his eye. It had almost been obscured by offers of penis enlargement and coupons for the Sportman's summer blowout.

From: Christian McGannon

Subject: Where are you?

Hey Finn,

I called your mother. Sorry if that's weird, man. The cohort was worried about you. Seems like we had reason to be. I didn't get much out of your roommate except for that you were going through some shit. Are you going to try to get back in? I bet you could test out if you do all the back-up. Three months isn't that long. Anyway, get back to me when you have time.

Good luck!

-Christian

Christian had been the closest thing Finn had to a friend in grad school. Not that they'd really hung out. But, he would sit next to him sometimes in class. To Finn, that had been really putting himself out there. He was ashamed he hadn't spared Christian one thought this whole time. Most likely, he'd forgotten about Finn by now.

Finn wanted to hope that what Christian was saying about testing back in was right. The email was a month old already, and even then Christian had made it sound like a bit of a long shot.

He nibbled on his bottom lip. What did he have to lose? Before Finn could chicken out, he typed out a quick response giving Christian his new phone number and saying that he was back and that he'd try to talk to the professors today. Almost immediately, his phone buzzed with an incoming text notification.

Dude, you're back on campus? Where? I'll come meet you.

Startled, Finn hesitated. Did he mean right now? He

should respond later. *Why? He wants to help you. He's your friend, right?* He could have friends. He was *good enough* for friends. Finn shoved a large amount of bagel in his mouth and tapped out his reply, pressing send and smearing a little cream cheese on his phone.

Fifteen minutes later, he spotted Christian ambling up the sidewalk. He smiled and looked really awake despite the early hour. His dirty blond hair was just long enough to bounce with each step, and his cheeks were rosy. Had it been a long walk? Finn stood once Christian was close, but he wasn't sure what to do next. A hug? Would that be weird? A handshake? People shook hands. That was a normal, acceptable social gesture.

He had his hand out, but Christian ignored it and pulled him into a hug. It lasted a little longer than Finn thought was socially acceptable and he held him kind of tightly. He never realized how strong Christian was. Still, Finn wasn't exactly the encyclopedia for what was socially acceptable, and he wasn't about to do something to make it all weird like pull away too early.

Christian released the hug but kept his hands on Finn's shoulders and stared as if scrutinizing him. Finn squirmed.

"Are you okay, man? You don't have to talk about it, but if you want to..." Christian made it clear by his tone that it was entirely Finn's choice.

Finn mumbled and cleared his throat. "Yeah, just going through some stuff. Maybe later we will get into it. Like... with beers." *With beers?* This is what he got for trying to sound like a guy's guy.

If Christian noticed, he didn't let on. "Yeah, sure, absolutely."

"What are you doing up so early?" Finn asked, desperate to fill the silence.

Christian gave him an easy smile. "I was at the gym. The pool is empty this early. Just about the only time it is."

Now that he mentioned it, Finn remembered that Christian had originally gotten into undergrad on a tennis scholarship. He didn't think that mattered once they'd gotten accepted into the graduate program, but that obviously didn't mean Christian had stopped playing or staying fit. Which he was. His body was tall and lean, but a muscled sort of lean. Not like Luke who was as sturdy as a body-builder—without the weird random muscles and bulgy veins.

Finn wasn't sure how to reply and thought he'd let too much time pass as he scrambled to think of one, so he started nodding exuberantly like he thought it was great that the pool was empty.

"So you're going to try to get back in? That's great. The hardest coursework has far and above been psychopathology, but really, you could write a series of papers to show your competency. Your biggest issue is going to be getting past Professor Paterson. As a teacher he is knowledgeable but since you left he's been appointed as psych department head. He's a bit of a stickler."

Christian blushed as if he'd said something far worse about the man who Finn remembered as a top-level dick. Finn smiled at the other man's slight embarrassment. So he wasn't the only one with words in his head that he didn't know how to say. Christian looked up then, his eyes on Finn's smile. He grinned and then reached his hand across the table, setting his warm palm on top of Finn's hand. The gesture was sweet and kind and nearly brought tears to Finn's eyes.

"It is really good to be sitting across from you. The cohort was—you know, scratch that. I don't know why I keep saying that. I was worried about you. Me. I thought, you blew it, buddy, that I'd lost my chance. And maybe I have, but you need to know, you have a friend and aren't alone in...this. Any of it. I'll help you out every step of the way. Hell, I'll start asking a million questions during lectures to slow our progress way down." He smiled at his joke, but Finn was still trying to blink back his tears. Christian's gaze wandered to a spot on the other side of the street. His smile dropped, and his eyes widened with what looked like fear.

"Do you know that guy?" he asked.

Finn turned.

The sight of Luke, glaring at them from across the street was like a punch to his gut and a tickle to his groin. How was he instantly so mad while also being turned on? Luke wore a tight black t-shirt and worn jeans that clung to his hips in a way that made Finn jealous of the denim. What gave him the right to look so angry and attractive?

"Yeah, uh," Finn's mouth felt dry. He licked his lips, trying to be able to speak again. Luke lasered in on his mouth. If possible, he looked angrier. "He's my sister's friend. He's crashing at her house right now too."

Luke's expression darkened further. Had he somehow heard Finn from across the street and then found fault in what he'd said? What did he expect Finn to say? He's the guy who just gave me two mind-blowing orgasms and then left before I could wake up? A rush of fury controlled Finn's next movements. He deliberately turned away from Luke, bringing his full attention to Christian.

"Don't worry, if we ignore him he might—" Before he finished Finn saw a shadow cast over their table. A long, domineering shadow.

Christian smiled, half standing, his tone placating. Of

course, he would try to diffuse the situation. "Hey, I'm Christian. One of Finn's—" he began with a tiny tremble in his words.

"I don't give a fuck who you are," Luke snarled.

Finn got to his feet abruptly. His chair hit the front of Luke's body, and when he stood and turned to face him, he was so close he could've kissed him without leaning forward. "Don't be a dick. What the hell are you even doing here?"

Luke leveled a domineering expression toward him. "Taking you home," he said, his words clipped.

Like a child? Like some wandering pet? Not like the lover he abandoned. Finn wanted to punch him so badly his knuckles itched. "Fuck off."

CHAPTER FIVE

Luke was being an asshole. He knew it. But, after the talk he'd had with Daryl, he'd rushed home in a frenzy. The urge to see Finn and claim him all over again had been too strong. And then, he'd been gone. Panic had clawed at him and did not release his heart until Luke had tracked Finn's scent all the way across town to the sleepy cafe on the corner. His relief had been short-lived when he saw that his Finn wasn't alone. Not by a long shot.

Fueled by rumors and what-ifs, by the horror stories Daryl had seemed to have gotten a perverse pleasure in relaying to Luke, he'd stalked over to his mate, ready to tear the challenger apart. Stories of mates who hadn't been claimed securely, stolen by someone stronger or better, stories of mates who hadn't been protected and had been killed, leaving the wolf to grow insane in their absence, all swirled in his mind.

The most important thing Daryl had said was that the mating connection could be tenuous at first and that it really wasn't secure until one of the party had conceived.

All of this combined was why, when that little shit had

dared to put his hand on Luke's mate, he'd seen red. And then, to make it all worse, his Finn had turned *away* from him.

He wasn't turned away from him now. Oh no, he was deliciously, cock throbbingly close. Luke had to fight his primal urge to bend Finn over where he stood to show that little prick across the table who Finn belonged to.

But he doesn't belong *to you. Not yet.* One fuck did not a mating make. At least, not in Finn's head, obviously.

And then, by shifter standards, he couldn't ever be Luke's. Though, Luke had already pretty much sent that notion straight to hell where it belonged. Finn was his mate. He just needed to convince Finn of that.

He would. They'd have a lengthy, reasonable discussion. At a later date. Right now, Luke just needed to get Finn out of this situation. Get him alone in a place where he could smell only him, feel him and be soothed by his nearness.

"Come on, Finn. We're going."

"Like hell," Finn spat.

Why was his mate fighting him now of all times? Why was it making him a thousand times hornier? Luke took a grounding breath. "Finn, I just need you to—"

"He-he said he doesn't want to go with you," the other guy said.

Luke sort of respected him. The guy sounded terrified but was still trying to protect Finn. Too bad Finn wasn't his to protect. "If I were you, I would shut the fuck up and walk away from this," Luke said, putting enough growl behind it to ensure his meaning was clear.

Finn stood straighter like he was protecting the other guy. That just pissed Luke off while simultaneously turning him on more. He liked seeing this sort of fire in his mate. "I don't understand this new attitude of yours, but Christian is my friend, and you don't get to talk to him like that." Finn turned from Luke again, but this time just his head rotated away. His body stayed in line with Luke's. Chest to chest. Hip to hip. "I'm sorry about this. I'll call you?"

"Are you sure?" Christian asked, clearly unhappy that he was being dismissed.

"Yeah." Finn turned from Christian to look at Luke directly in the eyes with a challenging stare. "I'll deal with this."

Luke's wolf howled.

Once Christian had taken his leave, Luke found that he could breathe a little deeper, his claws felt a little less likely to break through the skin at his fingertips.

That was until Finn wheeled on him, shoving him back with enough strength that he almost stumbled. He did take a step back though so his mate wouldn't feel like his efforts were fruitless.

"I don't have any idea what your fucking problem is but you will never be that rude to him again. Do you hear me? He is like, my only fucking friend and I don't need some guy who came in my ass once to stomp around thinking he has some claim on me. I especially don't need you running around spouting your mouth off and scaring him away. Christian is going to help me get my life back on track, and you will not mess this up for me. Get it?" He lurched forward so that they were literally nose to nose. "Get it?"

Luke wanted to kiss Finn so badly his lips tingled, but he thought that might get him a knee in the crotch. So, instead, he just closed his eyes and inhaled his mate's angry, sexy scent. It helped in some ways and made other things worse.

"Are you smelling me?"

Luke opened his eyes. Finn stared at him with an expression that was intrigued and weirded out. *You need to control yourself.* He took a step away and nodded, no use denying it now. "Yes I am, and yes I get it. Can we go back home now?"

Finn cast his eyes around as if trying to find a reason why he couldn't. "I guess yeah, but I'm walking, and I like to walk alone."

Luke smiled. He almost managed to make it not look bitter. "It's the only way I walk."

Pain, or maybe the recognition of pain flashed behind Finn's beautiful brown eyes. "I guess you could like, walk behind me or something. At a distance. Like, a few steps back."

Luke bowed his head in agreement. All that meant was that he would have an unfettered view of Finn's ass the entire way back. He waved his arm to the side in a sweeping gesture. Finn grabbed his paper coffee cup and the rest of his bagel. He stopped short. "Do you want anything?" he asked in a mumble.

Honestly, Luke was all coffee'd out. He shook his head.

Finn slid the bagel in the paper parchment pouch it had come in and with coffee in hand and head held high, he led the way back home.

FINN THOUGHT they'd been walking for about a mile and true to his word, Luke stayed a few steps behind. He'd spent the first half trying to catch Luke staring at his butt. He was sure the guy was, but every time he turned back, Luke's eyes were up, looking into Finn's with a challenge behind them.

The new information from Christian was in his mind,

but he kept getting distracted by Luke, specifically all the odd things that had happened concerning him.

"How did you find me?" Finn asked, facing forward and in a tone that was quiet for polite conversation.

"You mean at the cafe?" Luke answered as if it was perfectly normal that he'd heard Finn's question clearly.

Finn filed that bit of new information away. "Yeah, I didn't say anything about it, not even to Frannie."

"I got lucky?"

"Are you asking me?"

"No. I just don't want to lie, and I'm trying to make this...there are a few things...and well, we should talk, but... hey, your house is the other way." Luke took a few long strides so that he walked beside Finn.

"I know. I decided I needed to go to the library. Frannie's is just that way." Finn pointed, but when Luke stayed beside him, he stopped. "You don't have to come with me. It will be really boring."

"The library is pretty far though."

"I know how to get back to Frannie's from the library."

"I like being around you," Luke said, and his words sounded so honest that even Finn could find no doubt in them. "Besides, I—uh—need to go to the library too. There is a book I wanted."

Finn shuffled, not sure how to say what he needed to say while knowing it needed to be said. Luke was older than him, by probably ten years or so and he seemed like the type of guy who had known who and what he was from the womb. And he made no apologies for it. Finn, on the other hand, couldn't *stop* saying sorry.

"I apologize to tables when I run into them," Finn blurted.

Luke laughed. It did amazing things to his already gorgeous face.

"That wasn't supposed to be funny. I'm trying to warn you away. You know what you are. I don't. I'm still trying to figure out *why* I am, much less who. I know I am twenty-fucking-five and should have a better grasp on all of this. But—is this making any sense? I had an amazing time last night. That only fills me with more questions."

Luke let his fingers brush Finn's softly, almost interlocking. Finn found it was hard to breathe. "I did too," Luke said, unashamed.

A car passed and Finn jerked his hand back, shoving it in his pocket. "I wasn't lying, Luke, when I said that was my first time. I didn't know that I was, that I could want...I still don't know if I am—I mean, probably I am?" He felt flustered and was confusing himself.

Luke didn't look flustered though. He looked calm and sure. "Do you have to put a label on it? Why can't you be Finn who enjoys having mind-blowing sex with Luke?"

Finn blinked at him. "I have to go to the library."

"Did I say the wrong thing?" Luke asked, keeping in step with him.

"I don't even know if I'm that much. What if I'm only Finn who enjoyed that one night with Luke?" He expected Luke to stop then, once he thought he wasn't getting any more out of the situation.

He didn't. His steps never even faltered. His responding words were even and confident. "That would be fine, for now. But I would eventually convince you otherwise."

This time, Finn did doubt him. Not because there was a sudden lack of sincerity in his words, but because it didn't make a damn ounce of sense. He watched the street idly as it filled with more cars as the morning progressed.

Maybe, Finn wondered, he was a really great lay? Funny, none of the girls he'd ever had sex with had seemed all that impressed. Of course, every single one of those times he'd been drunk or under some other chemical influence. He actually couldn't remember a single one of their names. Finn scowled. Did that make him a slut?

"*What* are you thinking?" Luke asked, bringing him back to the present.

Finn shook his head. No way was he going there. "If you're coming, let's go. The library is just about to open." He resumed his course, not sure if Luke was going to follow, but sort of hoping he would.

A FEW HOURS later and Finn had a pile of books that he could reasonably hide behind. Good thing since Luke had a habit of just staring at him for long periods of time.

Was this how Luke would convince him they were supposed to have sex again? By awkward-ing his clothes off? He wished Frannie would hurry up and come home from her retreat. Finn had a thousand questions about how she had met Luke, how he ended up crashing at her house and what was up with his superpowers.

As if riding his background information train of thought, Luke leaned forward and whispered, "So, that guy at the cafe, he's a buddy of yours, you said?"

Finn narrowed his eyes at Luke, still pissed at how he'd acted toward Christian. "Yes. We were in the same group of students going through grad school at the same time. The same group I am trying to get back into, with Christian's help. I didn't realize we were friends until recently. He is a really great guy."

Luke growled at that, but there wasn't much menace in it. It almost sounded involuntary. Still, the librarian shot them a warning glance.

Finn opened his mouth to relieve his worries but what would he say? *You have nothing to worry about? I've been in the same classes with Christian for years, and you were still my first?* He didn't have the balls to say any of that, and it seemed a little presumptive of him. He didn't know if Christian liked him like that. Finn just closed his mouth instead.

"I wish you would say the words inside of you," Luke said.

Finn's brow furrowed.

"At least with me, anyway," he amended.

Finn scooped his books up. Luke lunged forward like he wanted to take them from him, but Finn stopped him with a warning glare. He could carry his own books, thank you. "I thought you said you needed a book?" Finn reminded him.

"Yeah," Luke said, and without looking, he grabbed the nearest book from the closest shelf. "Here it is."

Finn leaned forward to see the title and grinned. "How to Find Your Inner Goddess?"

Luke glanced at the book in his hands and then gave Finn a smile that was all teeth. "She's in here somewhere."

Finn's head fell back and his mouth opened as he laughed so hard and loud he couldn't control it. His body shook as he tried to quiet himself. It felt amazing. When he finally calmed enough to check his books out the librarian seemed relieved that they were leaving. It turned out, Luke didn't even have a library card, and he tried to put the book back on the shelf, but Finn checked it out for him. After all, who was he to stand between Luke and his inner goddess?

When they exited the library, the sun had risen high into the sky, and it had warmed considerably. By the time they'd reached Frannie's house, Finn was sweating under the pile of books. He opened the door, ostensibly ignoring Luke's attempt to help him. He stepped through the entryway and into the living room.

The space had been cleaned, he'd noticed that earlier and assumed Luke had done it. There was an empty spot where the coffee table had been. Earlier in the morning, Finn had nearly sprinted past this room, now he stood, stuck between an empty space and a strong man. He stared at the spot where the coffee table had been, the one they'd smashed the night before. Finn felt like his eyes were glued to the spot. Its emptiness was a beacon, proof of what had happened.

"If you want to take a shower, I can—" Luke stopped talking when he almost ran into Finn's backside.

Finn was stuck. He felt Luke settle into the space behind him. His warm breath was a constant tickle at Finn's neck. Then, light as a butterfly's wing, he felt Luke's lips at his neck—in the exact spot Finn had been touching before. It was just a light kiss now, so why did Finn suddenly wish Luke would throw him down, mount him and bite him at that spot again? He hissed at the images flashing through his brain.

"Go, take a shower," Luke ordered, his voice strained. "Maybe after we can rent a movie? Too hot of a day to do anything else."

Absently, he was aware of Luke taking the books from his hands, pushing him lightly down the hallway and into the bathroom. Then, Luke shut the door, letting Finn have a desperately needed moment alone.

CHAPTER SIX

LUKE SET the stack of books down neatly on the dining table in the kitchen. He fought his natural instinct to turn and go back to his mate. How had any mated wolf gotten anything done? Luke had been sporting his hard-on from the moment he'd spotted Finn's backside, bent over, reading his sister's note. Fucking him hadn't eased it. Something told him that seeking his own release probably wouldn't do any good either. Hell, it might make it worse. He grimaced. Luke, the big bad alpha wolf, was afraid to jerk himself off.

It had taken all his power to send Finn away to a different room to be naked and horny on his own. And Finn was definitely both of those things. The scent of his arousal had punched Luke right in the face. But the longer he spent with Finn, the more he learned about him, and Luke knew already that his Finn wasn't the type to be endlessly led by his dick. He wasn't comfortable with hurried or rash decisions. If he wanted any measure of success, Luke needed to ease Finn into the idea of being his mate, into the idea of Luke being a shifter. He needed to go slowly. Romance him.

Despite his recent behavior, Luke knew he could be

suave. Granted, he had lived a lot of his life on the fringes of society, never welcomed in a pack, never feeling all the way comfortable with normal humans. His time in well-populated areas was limited to short trips made out of necessity. Frannie had been camping in the middle of nowhere when they had met, and she'd invited him back. He would have to thank her again for that. And for being so cool about him being a shifter. Writers were awesome like that.

But, she hadn't been the first person to invite him into their home. Luke had always found it enjoyable, getting to know a person just as long as he could bail when things got too permanent. He'd even dated, mostly other lone wolves or the occasional human. Once, he'd even dated a lion shifter. Luke snorted, moving the first book on the pile so that it lined more evenly with the rest of the stack. That had been his shortest relationship ever. But the point was Luke could date. He had moves. He could be smooth.

In the bathroom, the water shut off. Luke imagined Finn standing in the shower, reaching for a towel, drips of water sliding down his skin. The little droplets of water would be like tiny roller coaster cars traversing down the edges of his muscled body.

Luke wanted to lick him dry. He wanted his tongue all over his mate's skin, tasting every inch of him. Then, he would nibble and suck and mark him so that everyone who saw would know to stay the fuck away. They'd know that Finn was his and they had better fucking—

Luke stopped short. He'd moved out of the kitchen and down the hallway without noticing. Now, he stood on the other side of the bathroom door, his hand outstretched as if to yank the handle open.

This would not do. He'd only scare Finn this way. He backed up quickly. The bathroom door clicked open the moment he got to the end of the hallway. Luke reversed his momentum and lurched a foot forward like he'd just started walking down the hall. Finn stepped out, dressed in loose sweatpants and a faded blue and white baseball tee.

"Oh, hey, you're done," he said casually. Too casually. "So, I was thinking we could go get a movie, maybe? There is one of those DVD/Blue-ray vending machines up the street at the mini-mart. Maybe order in after?" Luke should kick himself. These were his moves? Super slick. Not.

But there was something about Finn that made him not want to use practiced moves that he'd used on another guy. Finn was special, he deserved an authentic Luke.

"Great, good idea," Finn said, reaching for a baseball cap. "There is this vegan place that opened while I was in treatment that I have been dying to try."

Luke grimaced. If that was what his mate wanted. His stomach twisted at the thought of eating nuts and soy pressed and twisted into only the shape of delicious, juicy meat.

Finn had slid his gray cap on so Luke didn't see his grin for a few seconds. When he spotted it, he smiled. "You're joking?" he asked, his stomach needing to be absolutely sure.

"Yes, I am joking. Frannie orders out all the time so there should be a stack of menus by the fridge. Go pick one, and I'll grab my shoes."

Fuck it all if joking and discussing the day's plans didn't feel like the most natural thing in the world. In the past, this would've been when Luke's legs would have itched to move on, to find the next thing. Now though, even the quiet walk to the mini-mart felt so perfectly normal that Luke had to keep stopping himself from casually reaching over and grabbing Finn's hand. Going slow might kill him, but if it helped his mate, he would die happy. When they got to the mart, they stood in front of the touch screen that displayed all of the newest releases.

FINN WAS sad when they got to the mini-mart. The walk had been *that* perfect. Amiable silence wrapped up in a beautiful day. He almost suggested they keep walking, but how could he spin that so he didn't sound like a lonely weirdo desperate for just a few more moments of perfect communal silence?

At the kiosk he swung back, waiting for Luke to take charge and choose a movie for the two of them. But Luke just stood there, looking back at Finn expectantly.

Anxiety threatened to flood his head. *What is your problem, Finn? It is a movie. You can make this one choice without having a meltdown.* But he wasn't sure he could. It was little moments like this where he truly failed at acting normal.

"I don't know what you've seen," he said.

"Not a lot." He flashed Finn a conspiratorial sort of smile.

Finn tried to return it. "More than me probably. The last four months anyway." His lips fell, the smile vanishing. Why would he make a joke that reminded Luke that he just got out of an institution? That he wasn't the average guy he'd done an alright job of pretending to be? He didn't dare look at Luke again. He couldn't stand the judgment he knew would be there.

Finn had grown used to getting that face from everyone else, but he couldn't bear to get it from Luke. Not when he enjoyed his lust-filled expressions so much more.

"Hey," Luke said sharply, hooking a finger under his

chin and jerking his face so that he had to look at him. "It's okay, Finn. With me, you are always okay."

As if not horrified enough, Finn blushed. He was sure it was the deepest most glaring shade of tomato red. "I'm sorry, I don't want to say the wrong thing."

"I told you already, I want to hear what is in your head. Don't hide your words from me."

He nibbled at his bottom lip thoughtfully. Luke's dark eyes zeroed in on the movement. For a crazy moment Finn thought Luke might kiss him, but then he released his face. "Let's choose something so we can order, I'm starving."

Finn studied the screen, scrolling past a handful of movies, looking for one that caught his eye. He wouldn't over-analyze it. He would just wait for the—

"Oh! I remember hearing about this one when I went in, Silver Moon, Blood Moon. I thought it looked..." He was immediately distracted by Luke's response. An expression of amusement and absolute horror was on his face. "You've seen it?" Finn guessed.

Luke looked like he was biting his cheeks to keep from laughing. What was so funny?

"No, I've never seen that one. I don't usually watch shifter propaganda," he said finally.

"Huh? You don't watch what?"

"Nothing, we should get it."

Finn had clicked on the more information tab. "And, bonus, it has Scott Fusterson." A quick laugh escaped his lips. "Frannie calls him Scott Fuckmesohard. He must have worked out nonstop for this role—"

"Or we could get a different movie?" Luke nearly growled.

Finn smiled at the noise—a true, pure, peace-filled smile. He was beginning to really like that growling noise

Luke did all the time. "No, this is the one. And we should order Korean fried chicken when we get back. It has been forever since I've had some good Korean fried chicken." He almost winced and waited for Luke's disinterest or annoyance.

Luke just smiled, flashing those dimples. "If that's what you want, let's do it."

CHAPTER SEVEN

LUKE WAS the closest to heaven he'd ever been. The entire week he'd spent in his mate's company, except for the time Finn had left to have lunch with his mother. He returned to Luke a little weary and sad, but it hadn't taken Luke long to get him back in good spirits.

A lot of the time, Finn studied. He had some pretty important tests coming up but first, needed the university's permission to take them.

Luke found he didn't mind what he was doing or that Finn was doing something that didn't involve him exactly, he just enjoyed being near him, in the same room. He was even content to just exist in the same house together.

Luke studied Finn as Finn studied to get back into grad school. Each moment was a chance to learn more and more about his mate. For instance, Finn had a penchant for monster movies. Particularly werewolves. It had amused Luke at first, but he did grow irritated at the way Finn would drool over the pansy actors who were just pretending to be shifters.

The two of them sat on Frannie's large sectional, a bowl

of popcorn in the space between them watching one of those movies.

The actor on screen was doubled over in pain, the crunching and snapping of bones blared through the speakers as the actor shifted from human to wolf with the help of computer graphics and prosthetics.

Luke rolled his eyes. The dude was carrying on like a baby, whimpering and sputtering.

"What? Too scary?" Finn asked, one eye on the screen, one on Luke.

"Hmph. Yeah right."

Finn's eyes didn't return to the television screen. Instead, he stared at Luke, expectantly. Luke could appreciate that his mate was more forward with him now but also felt like he'd really stepped in it. Finn wasn't stupid, and Luke hadn't monitored what he was saying closely enough.

When Luke had woken up that morning, he hadn't planned on it being the day Finn found out he was a shifter.

What the hell was he supposed to say? *That's not how you shift?* Why couldn't he say that? Finn would have to know eventually what Luke was.

"Actually, Finn, shifting into a wolf—"

"Would be awful."

Luke closed his mouth.

"Being a wolf wouldn't be so bad. But, to have a secret like that, one that was harder to hide. I don't think I would want to live like that."

Luke felt the shaky ground he was on. He wasn't lying, except by omission. "Would you feel like you had to hide it? Couldn't you trust the people close to you enough to tell them?"

Finn thought about that. "Sometimes, secrets are a burden." His eyes opened wide as if he couldn't believe what he had said. Luke moved the popcorn bowl and sat nearer to him, needing to be closer to his mate while he could sense he was in distress. "I can't believe I said that."

"Why?"

Finn reached for the popcorn bowl. He was actively trying to put barriers between them. Luke knew it would make him more comfortable, but he still couldn't allow it. "Talk to me, Finn. What secrets do you have that are a burden?" He reached across and grabbed his hand, pulling his arm to the space between them and turning his wrist scar side up.

Finn flinched when he saw it and tried to pull his hand back. "Does it have something to do with this?"

"*That* was an accident." He sounded defensive and something else.

He tensed at the way Finn emphasized *that*. Luke's wolf raged at the implication even while he didn't one hundred percent believe him. His wolf wanted to howl in the air, scratch, and paw at the ground. Outwardly, Luke could just sit and try to look like he was remaining calm. There was no tangible entity for him to defeat that would save his mate, nothing Luke could simply sink his teeth into and make better. Right now, Finn's mind was his greatest enemy, and that was a battleground that Luke was still ill-equipped to fight on.

"The year before," Finn spoke as if in a daze, "there wasn't some big catalyst or anything. I just, got really drunk one night and gave it a try. Took a handful of sleeping pills. Woke up the next morning covered in vomit. Showered, went to class."

That was it. He'd said it all so matter of factly as if the entire world hadn't almost been irrevocably altered. As if

Luke hadn't come painfully close to losing his mate before they'd even met.

"Does that make me weak?" The question was so quiet he almost didn't hear it.

"Weak?" Luke's throat was so dry he barely got the word out. "No."

Finn actually smiled but not for long. "I don't think it feels good finally telling someone, but it feels...something. I'm sorry to burden you like this."

Luke almost snorted. Finn wouldn't have understood the meaning behind it.

"If you need to even the field, burden me..." Finn said.

Luke was too busy containing his wolf. He felt like a bomb had been dropped on him and he couldn't get the mental image out of his head. His Finn had almost been taken from him. Luke's purpose and contentment, all the happiness he'd experienced since knowing him had almost never existed.

He needed to touch Finn, to feel him and know he was alive, with him and safe. Slowly, he cupped Finn's face with his hands. He had to go slow to keep control and to not frighten his mate.

Finn's eyelids fluttered, but he kept them on him. His soulful brown eyes seemed like they could see through Luke straight into his heart, his soul. Luke covered his mouth with his own. It was a deliberate kiss, each movement measured and decided upon. Luke needed to be careful, be—

Finn moaned and then sank his teeth into Luke's lower lip, and Luke snapped. He launched forward, pushing his mate onto his back while grinding his pelvis against him. They were both fully clothed, a fact that Luke wholeheartedly despised. His dick strained out against its confines. He felt Finn's cock pressing up as well. That realization had him grinning.

"I like the way your smile feels on my mouth," Finn said, breaking the kiss to do so. He reached up and got two handfuls of Luke's hair, yanking his face back down so that his lips crashed against his mouth again.

Luke speared Finn's mouth with his tongue. It had been too long since he'd tasted his mate and now he wasn't sure if he could ever stop. At least it didn't seem like Finn wanted him to. He squirmed and wiggled under him, thrusting his hips upward against Luke's erection. With each jolt of contact, Finn made tiny noises in the back of his throat that Luke found as hot as they were adorable.

Luke shifted, raising his upper half so that he was on his knees straddling Finn's body. Finn sat up as he did so. Luke reached for the hem of his own shirt, pulling it up, breaking their kisses long enough to yank it over his head. He tossed it aside and then did the same thing to Finn's shirt. He tore his lips away and sat back.

Finn exhaled sharply, a noise that told Luke he was unhappy with the direction things had gone. But how could Luke resist taking this moment to just watch his sexy mate? He was sitting vertically, propped up on his elbows. His chest rose and fell with his heavy breath, his skin shone with a beautiful rosy flush. Finn's brown eyes had turned nearly black with lust.

Luke imagined his own expression was similar. He kept appreciating Finn's physique, letting his gaze travel lower. He had a naturally lean muscle tone. His biceps flexed with the effort of holding himself up under Luke's weight. His abdominal muscles rippled and clenched. Luke's gaze went even lower, admiring his lean hips and the way his muscles streamlined, acting like an arrow, tempting and guiding Luke's gaze down.

Weak? His mate was definitely not that.

"I don't want you to hurt yourself again," Luke ordered, his tone gruff. To ease the aggression in his words, he undid Finn's pants and moved over to slide them down and off his body. He almost got distracted when Finn's dick sprang up in his face, but Finn hadn't responded yet. "Promise me, you won't hurt yourself like that again." He stroked Finn's cock lazily, downward and then when he reached the base, he took his hand away, only to start again at the tip. "Finn." He took his hand away entirely, and Finn actually whined.

So fucking hot.

"Never again." He gripped the shaft at the base with a hold that was tight.

"No, never again," Finn whimpered.

"You come to me if you need to talk something out, got it? No matter what it is." He took Finn in his mouth, letting his tongue lick his cock, enjoying the taste and feel of him.

"Yes, whatever you say, please, just don't stop." Finn returned his hands to Luke's head. He didn't guide Luke's mouth but tugged at his hair, showing Luke how he liked to be licked. "Fuck, your mouth is amazing," he hissed.

Luke tickled Finn's thigh. His fingers crept higher and higher until they danced outside his puckered entrance. He stopped though. Normally, Luke didn't worry about lube. He had either his cum or his tongue but his mouth was busy and this moment was for Finn.

Finn noticed his hesitation and oddly, he blushed. He reached under the cushion and produced a small clear bottle. "I, uh, hid it there just in case."

"You dirty slut," Luke said with a smile. As long as Finn

was just his slut, he didn't mind. Didn't mind was an understatement, it made him horny as hell. Well, hornier.

Luke worked a small amount of the lubricant out of the bottle and used the tip of his finger to massage around his hole making Finn mumble sexy half sentences. Luke couldn't remember being more content. His mate's dick in his mouth and his fingers in his mate's ass. Finn moaned and jerked down, sliding Luke's finger all the way in.

"Oh, yes, please," he begged.

Fucking his mate with his finger, Luke waited for the passage to relax enough before he added another finger. He was rewarded by a burst of Finn's flavor, salty and earthy, full of life. His mate bucked up and screamed in pleasure. He hastened the pace of his bobbing head, loving the sensual squeaking that flooded his ears. When he heard the squeaks reach their peak, he crooked his finger in a come hither motion, brushing against Finn's g-spot as his mouth became a vacuum on his dick. Instantly, spurts of come splashed Luke's tongue. He sucked it down, keeping up the massage until he sucked the very last drop. He took his fingers out, and Finn whined like he missed the feeling. His eyes were closed though, and Luke knew well enough what to expect. His mate liked to sleep after sex. Luke's cock was hard as steel now, but it didn't matter. Now and always, Finn would come first.

Luke brought the glass of water to his mouth. Finn was still asleep, and Luke had spent the last two hours warring with himself inside the kitchen. He wanted nothing more than to slide in bed beside Finn, but he wasn't sure of what Finn would do if he woke up with Luke there. His inner wolf demanded he go to his mate now, claim him again and again until there was no choice, no discussion of where Luke would sleep. His wolf was a dick though, and Luke wasn't sure if Finn would appreciate him in his bed or if it would weird him out.

Luke stared through the kitchen window to the dark yard. The night sky was cloudy, not that there were many stars to see within the city limits anyway. Luke could see his reflection in the window. He wore red plaid boxers and a white t-shirt. His dick stuck out from his body, still hard but he had accepted that as its regular state now.

He set the glass down on the counter and turned to go down the hallway, still unsure of which room he would go into. Just as he turned, he caught movement outside in the corner of the dark yard. A shadowy shape skulking at the edge of his vision. Luke suppressed his growl. The form came closer, approaching the sliding glass door in the dining area. Whoever it was, knew where the motion detecting lights were installed.

Luke shifted, his clothes splitting and falling off as his body fluidly reformed itself. Momentarily, he pondered on how wrong the movies had gotten it. Shifting wasn't painful, it wasn't a breaking of bones, it was fluid and seamless. He sniffed the air with his wolf nose and pawed across the kitchen. The sliding door opened. He caught sight of something silver in the intruder's hand and licked his chops in anticipation. If this thing thought it would enter into the house of his mate uninvited and keep its life, it was dead wrong.

Luke leaped, a quiet snarl ripped from him despite his attempt to stay completely silent. The truth was, it had been too long since he shifted and he was probably a little over excited. He landed on top of the intruder, his teeth finding the soft skin at the intruder's neck. One bite was all it would take.

"Stop," a squeaky girl's voice said. "Luke! It's me!"

His blood ran cold. He had been milliseconds from chomping down on his friend's neck. On his mate's sister's neck. He leaped off and stayed in wolf form. He'd be naked when he shifted, and he was too embarrassed to look at Frannie with his human face. He should have smelled her, recognized her scent. He was too keyed up in the moment to think logically like that. He watched Frannie sit up, rubbing her neck. She was curvy with a mess of curly brown hair on the top of her head that almost always looked disheveled. She had Finn's eyes, though hers were a little darker brown.

"Cheese and rice, Luke! Didn't you hear me coming around the side?"

Luke shook his wolf head.

"Where is Finn?"

Was there worry in her voice? Did she think he had hurt himself? Worse, that Luke had hurt him? He growled softly and nodded his head back, indicating the hallway and room beyond.

She looked relieved. "You two are getting along then? Can't imagine why not, it is hard to dislike Finner. Was that my coffee table in the trash out there?"

Luke was endlessly happy he'd stayed in wolf form. He moved over to act as a brace to help Frannie to her feet. She walked with him through the kitchen, and they entered the living room together.

"A new table? What happened to the old one? Is that your underwear?" She reached forward to grab Finn's underwear that Luke had taken off him earlier. Luke lunged and grabbed it from her with his teeth. "Why is there a bottle of...Oh. My. God."

Luke sat back on his haunches as far from her on the couch as was possible. Still, her hand snaked out and smacked him hard on his side.

"He is my brother you fucking horny animal! He is sensitive! How dare you!"

Luke let her get it out, but he would not let her think that he was using her brother. He mouthed her arm, not putting any pressure behind the bite, but the feel of his teeth against skin shocked her enough that she stopped.

It didn't stop her scowl. "Don't look at me like that, Luke! What do you expect me to think? I left you with my sweet brother for less than a week and come back to lube and undies. I've never even seen Finn kiss anyone before. I didn't even know he was gay. And you are a bit of a, well, he isn't as reckless with that kind of stuff as you are."

Luke growled. Frannie's eyes widened but more in surprise than fear. "What? You're offended? You expect me to believe that it isn't just a fling for you? That you've developed some sort of bond?"

Luke was about to shift so he could tell her exactly that when they were interrupted.

"What the hell is happening?" Finn asked with a sleepy voice that sounded angry and confused. "What the fuck, Fran?" There was fear in his voice when he finally saw Luke. He was larger than a normal wolf, probably looked more like a bear sitting on the couch like a human would. But, there wasn't an ounce of fear in Frannie, so he seemed to relax enough to go from scared to insanely suspicious. "I mean, seriously..."

"Uh," Frannie started, her eyes wide, her curly hair wild around her face. "So, he doesn't...uh."

"Fran, you are talking to a dog. Where is Luke? Did you hit your head?"

Wordlessly, Luke shifted back into his human form. He stood, naked from head to toe, not caring that Frannie was in the room. He only had eyes for his mate.

"Luke?" Finn said, his expression shuttered.

He took a step toward Finn, but Finn scrambled back like Luke was made of acid.

"What the—" Finn started but then stopped. It was as if he couldn't take his eyes off of Luke, but not in a good way, in a shocked, disbelieving and betrayed way.

"Let me explain," Luke tried, Finn silenced him with a sharp gesture, his hand slicing through the air.

"I told you things about me that...no one...and you couldn't find time in the week we were together...I mean really together to tell me? And *Frannie* knows?"

Was that where the anger came from, that his sister knew something before him? No, his mate wasn't fickle like that.

"Finners, it's not a big deal—"

"It fucking is, Francesca," Finn cut her off. Luke appreciated her attempt to help but thought it might be best if she was just quiet.

"You," he wheeled on Luke, pointing at him. "I opened up to you, trusted you. Gave you..." He looked so close to crying it killed Luke, he took another step toward him.

"Don't touch me, don't fucking come near me." He stumbled back as if he didn't trust Luke enough to stay away as he asked. With a wild turn, he sprinted down the hall, into his room, and slammed the door.

CHAPTER EIGHT

"Library is closing in fifteen minutes," the librarian reminded Finn as she walked by the desk he'd been sitting at for the better part of the day. Not like he didn't know what time the library closed.

She wanted to be sure though, so the librarian—he had learned her name was Pamela not because she told him or anything—reminded him every night. She'd been less than happy to see him back the first day, probably remembering how loud he'd been. But every day he showed, she frowned a little less.

A week of studying later and Pamela almost didn't scowl when she saw him come in. That practically made her Finn's best friend. She wasn't willing to keep the library open any later than nine though. They weren't *that* close.

Finn began to pack his stuff up. Pentmiller's Guide to Clinical Research went into the bag along with his outline and the notes Christian had sent him. He was slow to zip his bag up and when he finally did, chose to check his *gas station* phone before leaving. He saw the usual calls and texts. Some from Frannie, a couple from his mom and a lot from Luke the lying wonder. There was one text from Christian asking how he was getting along. Finn contemplated responding. He hadn't spoken to Christian face to face since that day at the cafe. He'd emailed Finn his notes. Part of Finn was insecure about what he would say if he started an actual conversation with Christian, but most of him knew that a talk with Christian would eventually turn into discussing the big bull-headed bully from the cafe and Finn didn't think he could talk about Luke. Not right now. Maybe never.

It wasn't that Luke had lied. After all, Finn had never asked him, are you a guy who can turn into a huge dog thing? But he had allowed Luke access to his body and mind on a level that no one ever had, and on a level Luke obviously hadn't wanted to reciprocate.

Pamela walked by again, making sure he was getting ready to leave. Christian's notes had been really helpful. Finn gave the librarian a small smile. Finn felt obligated to at least thank Christian.

Pamela would have to watch out, her top spot as number one friend might be in jeopardy.

Hey man, he typed, those notes were amazing. Thanks.

A few minutes passed, Finn was out of his chair, slow walking out of the library when he felt his phone vibrate.

Glad they could help, bud. What are you doing right now? Want to meet for drinks?

Finn winced. He *had* planned on walking as slow as could be considered forward movement back to Frannie's house where he would wait outside until he was brave enough to speed walk to his bedroom silently.

He guessed maybe drinks wouldn't be worse than that. He'd been feeling a little twitchy these days anyway and spent most of his nights pacing the length of his room.

He texted back and waited for Christian to send him the address. With a goodbye nod to Pamela, who followed directly behind him, he left the library. She turned the main lights off and locked the door the exact moment it had swooshed closed. *Sheesh, Pam, have somewhere to be?*

Finn's phone had just started to vibrate, and he was looking down at it, which was why he didn't notice the large guy until he bumped into him.

"Watch where you're fucking going," a different guy from the one he'd bumped into snarled at him.

Finn looked at him, bewildered by his sudden anger. "I-I'm sorry," Finn said, mostly out of shock.

"Yeah, you are," the guy said, getting closer to Finn. He had dark features, and a weird-shaped nose like it had been recently broken and hadn't healed correctly. "Hey, do I know you?" he asked with narrowed eyes. Then he closed his eyes and inhaled.

No, not inhaled. He *sniffed.*

Finn took a stumbling step back. The man he had bumped into strode forward and caught him before he could fall. He wasn't beady-looking like his friend. In fact, he had an eerily handsome, movie star quality about him. Oddly, he reminded Finn of that actor, Fuckmesohard from that werewolf movie.

That isn't odd, Finn, you idiot. They were whatever Luke was, they had to be. A third guy joined them. As unbelievable as it was, Finn couldn't deny, this third one even looked like Luke, an older, tireder version anyway. He regarded Finn with a curious expression.

"Does my friend know you?" Fuckmesohard asked in a smooth, darkly dangerous tone.

Finn hoped they couldn't hear his rapidly beating heart. He leveled his chin and deepened his voice, doing his best growly Luke impersonation. "No, sorry man." He stepped back and away from them. Turning his back on the pack of men had been difficult. His instincts screamed danger, but guys like that could probably smell danger. They definitely smelled something on him.

"HEY, FINN!" Christian called to him from a corner table at the pub. He looked casual in a teal and black button-up and dark jeans. His sleeves were rolled up revealing a second sleeve of tattoos.

Finn bit his lip nervously and then tried to smile. A feat made difficult while his lip was between his teeth. Christian's smile faltered. Great, he'd seen Finn acting like a spaz. "Are you okay?" he asked when Finn had gotten to the table.

"Yeah, I'm fine."

"O-kay," he said slowly, disbelievingly looking Finn up and down once and then again. He turned his gaze out through the storefront window. "I mean, you have a type at least," he said like it was a joke, but he sounded a little too strained for the amusement to be real.

Finn followed his gaze. The group of guys he'd bumped into had followed him. They were at the bar across the street, taking up a table outside on the sidewalk. None of them stared at him as Luke had at the cafe. They all had a pint of beer in front of them, but they were still. Unnaturally still. The one that looked like a movie star saw Finn looking and gave a small, almost charming wave.

"I don't know those people," Finn said, thinking there was no way Christian would believe him.

"Really? They remind me of that other guy. Luke? Is he your boyfriend?" Christian asked with false disinterest.

Finn watched the group of guys perk up at the mention of Luke's name. Almost like they'd heard Christian, but that was impossible. Luke had good hearing, but even he couldn't hear something someone said in a separate building with a busy street between them. Maybe one of them could read lips? If Finn were braver, he would've mouthed, very slowly, for them to all fuck off.

"He's my roommate," Finn said finally. "I actually thought he had a thing for my sister."

"But he doesn't?" Christian asked.

This was the exact conversation he'd wanted to avoid. Somehow, he'd opened with it. "It doesn't matter," Finn said, willing it to be true. He was over it. He was over weird dog people and possessive glances and steely determined eyes that knew how to reach into your soul. "What are you drinking?"

Christian looked pleased to change the subject of conversation. "Old fashioned, I don't think you would like it."

"Why?"

"Not your style. You seem more like a Lynchburg Lemonade type of guy. I'll order you one. I've got this thing where I can guess people's drinks. That was one of the reasons I decided to pursue psychology in grad school."

"Because you can tell what type of martini someone will like? That isn't much of a foundation."

Christian shrugged good-naturedly. "As good a reason as any. So, will you let me? You can get the next round."

Finn nodded, and a few minutes later a yellowish drink was set before him. He took a long pull on the straw. The sweet and sour flavor was refreshing, and the bite of whiskey was just what he wanted to finish his sip. He looked up at Christian who stared at him with an expectant expression. "You have a gift. This is delicious."

Christian beamed. His eyes were a very nice slate color. His dirty blond hair looked styled today, pulled back and kept in place with gel. Finn reached forward and touched a strand to see if he was right. He froze, realizing what he was doing too late. Finn leaned back and away from the other man. He took another long pull.

"I'm sorry," Finn mumbled. Despite his embarrassment, he felt the pleasant haze of the alcohol numbing his senses. Absently, he thought that the alcohol was kicking in kind of fast.

"Don't worry about it," Christian said like he didn't mind. "So, are you ready to talk now? Or do you need another lemonade?" Christian said but then frowned. "I mean, that was a joke, I wouldn't ever get you drunk to take advantage of...shit. How did I get going on this?" He massaged his jaw. It looked like he hadn't shaved that day and a bit of blond stubble scratched his hand.

"You are cute when you're flustered, did you know?"

Christian threw his head back and laughed. The motion made his Adam's apple bob. "It doesn't take much, does it? You are a cheap date."

Finn took one more long pull on the straw. He recognized this as false alcohol induced bravery and didn't want it to dissipate. Though, it hadn't ever happened this fast before, or this completely.

"I'm serious about not trying to get you drunk. It is just me here. You don't have to be nervous."

Finn wanted to point out that he was always nervous.

"You don't have to prove anything to me or give me anything. I'm trying to say, Finn, I don't expect anything from you. I'm not helping you so that you will give me something back. I do want to be your friend, but I'm not demanding it or anything. Is that alright with you?"

Finn nodded but was inwardly mortified. Christian didn't deserve drunk-Finn who made bad choices.

"Cool, let me get you another one, and I can tell you the news about Professor Paterson."

Christian returned with a fresh drink for both of them. Then he told Finn the best news he'd heard all week; Professor Paterson was going to be taking a leave of absence, which meant, he shouldn't even be on the deciding board that chose whether or not Finn would be allowed back into the graduate program.

Finn had done his best to relax and enjoy the new company. He took much longer, sipping on his second drink but it didn't seem to help. His skin still felt overheated. He moved his arm so that it pressed against the glass of the storefront. The moan of pleasure at the cool glass against his heated skin was barely containable. His body fidgeted restlessly, unable to stay in one position for too long. All over, his skin felt itchy, though there was no concrete origin. Had he developed some new allergy to alcohol? He'd drunk it recently without effects. Maybe something in the lemonade?

Weirder than any of that was the nagging pulse of desire, like a red-hot ember from an old campfire that refused to extinguish. He wasn't sure, but it felt a lot like being turned on. Why though?

He eyed Christian with new lenses. He had a lithe, swimmer's body. With his tousled dirty blond hair, tanned skin and tattoos he looked like he would be perfectly at home on a surfboard on some beach.

But Finn liked them a little sturdier, with dark features and a growl that could turn him on in less than a second.

Without really meaning to, he looked outside, noticing that Fuckmesohard and his band of probably dog people were still outside, sucking down pints. Fuckmesohard had the dark features, yes, but he also had an aura about him that Finn didn't trust. He seemed the type that would ask for a sandwich and then after complain that you didn't make it fast enough.

Finn was so thirsty his throat ached. He took a very long swig from his glass, abandoning the straw. His skin seemed to grow instantly hotter. His heartbeat quickened like he had sprinted a mile. He was perspiring and didn't have a clue as to why. He just knew that if he swiped his forehead with his finger, it would come off wet.

He closed his eyes, thankful that the world wasn't spinning. So he wasn't blasted drunk at least. That was little comfort. His lungs screamed for more air, and he panted, trying to give them the oxygen they demanded. It was too fast, so he tried to slow his breathing, taking deep breaths in through his mouth. That had been a mistake. His nagging turned-on feeling morphed into a raging wave of uncontrollable horniness. He ached, in literal agony from the extent of his need to be filled. He found Christian with wide, terrified eyes.

LUKE SET down the thick manuscript. He'd agreed a long time ago to be an expert on all of Frannie's shifter romance books. He'd tried to tell her that no one in the mainstream actually knew shifters existed, so she didn't need an expert. After all, it wasn't like anyone would accuse her of getting it wrong, but she'd just looked at him with that squinty expression that told him she'd already moved on to something else in her mind, and he should just do it. It was the least he could do for a friend who never once asked him to pay any rent.

"Pay attention to how I describe the transition. I don't want it to sound inauthentic," she said from her spot on the opposite side of the couch. She painted her toenails while catching up on some god-awful singing show. Her phone rang, and she glanced at the ID. "It's Finn, you wanna answer it?" she asked like she was waving a bone in front of a mutt. Which, she was. She sighed. "I can just let it go to voicemail. He is mad at me still and—"

Luke got to his feet and yanked the phone out of her hand. He retreated to the hallway to answer it, allowing them both a fraction of privacy. "Hello?" he said, hoping he didn't sound too wolfy.

"Um, is this the right number? Frannie?" a worried male voice asked.

"This is her number, who is this?" Luke loathed whoever was on the other end of the line. He swallowed his growl. Why the hell did some other man have his mate's phone?

"Oh, you must be the roommate. Hey, we've met. Anyway, I don't know what is going on. Finn came down for some drinks, and now he is acting...strange."

"Where are you?" Luke barked.

The guy, Luke tried to remember his name, *Christian*, told him the name of the pub. "And, um, well, there are these guys outside too. Finn said he didn't recognize them, but—"

Luke swore, disconnecting the line and throwing the phone back to Frannie. She asked him something, but Luke couldn't stop. His mate was in danger.

Luke slowed his motorcycle down as he neared the pub. He felt the hairs on his neck rise. The place seemed to be crawling with shifters. Were they all here for his Finn? He parked his bike a block away, choosing to go the rest of the way on foot. He was surer that way. When he got to the block where the pub was, he cursed. Across the street, an entire pack of shifters loitered. He spotted his father in the middle and could only assume the pack leader was probably with him. And, he'd called what looked like to be most of his pack to join him. Why?

Luke put his head down, ignoring the curious onlookers. It was generally a bad idea to put two alphas within fighting distance. Luke wasn't here to fight unless he had to.

Inside the pub, he searched for Finn. There were plenty of other patrons, all completely oblivious to what happened around them. He felt his claws extend in his frustration. Finally, Christian came running toward him from the back of the pub.

"Thank God. He's gotten worse."

Luke's blood ran cold. He let the other man lead the way through the pub, down a small hallway that ended in a T. The door to the left went to the men's restroom and the door to the right the women's. He stepped into the bathroom, and the scent of arousal slammed into him. Immediately, he turned, pushing Christian back and out of the bathroom before using the garbage can to prop against the door.

He found Finn, crouched in the opposite corner like a frightened animal. He looked so fragile and vulnerable. There was no way Luke would be able to allow Christian inside while his mate was in this state.

He inhaled and his mate's need was so thick, it had a taste. It lined his mouth like a rich sauce. Finn was bent over, panting. He lifted his head when Luke took a step toward him. Finn straightened and jumped into the air in one fluid motion. He wound his arms and legs around Luke as he climbed up his body.

Despite the warmth of Finn's body, cold realization filled Luke. This was why the other alpha had ordered his entire pack around, why they were all skulking outside. They could smell Finn's need. If the pack master was unmated, he would be biologically required to at least be allured by the scent of Finn's heat.

But that didn't make sense for so many reasons. One, Finn wasn't a shifter and two, he was a man. Human males didn't go into heat, not like this. Not unless...

His wheels turned and turned until Luke wished he could run himself over with them. Had he done this to his mate? Had his sperm transformed him somehow? An alpha was a powerful thing and not just because they were predisposed to leadership. If Luke's theory was correct, then that also meant they were able to transform.

What did all this mean for his squirming mate who was clinging to his body, pressing his most urgent body parts against Luke?

"Finn, I am so sorry," Luke said.

"Apology accepted," Finn replied with pupils so wide Luke wasn't sure he could even see clearly. "Now fuck me. Please," he drew the word out on a long whine.

Luke groaned and bit his lip so hard he thought it would bleed. "Finn, honey, try to listen to me. I think your body is going through...some changes. I don't understand it entirely, but I can say you are not in your right mind right now. I can't take advantage of that. Don't you remember how mad you are at me?"

"Mmhmm," Finn said, nuzzling against Luke's neck.

It felt wonderful, Finn's lips brushing against Luke's soft, vulnerable skin. Finn slid down his body and reached for Luke's zipper. He wrapped his fingers around Luke's solid cock. Luke swallowed his groan.

"No, baby, no—"

In seconds Finn was on his knees, Luke's cock slid past his lips and down his throat. *Holy shit.* It was deep in there. Apparently the mating heat had also turned off any sort of gag reflex Finn might have had. Luke felt his shaft throb, a jet of liquid shot from the tip straight down Finn's throat.

The noise Finn made would give Luke a hard-on for a million years.

Carnal, basic and appreciative, Finn doubled his sucking efforts, and Luke had to use more alpha strength than he would've liked to try to pry his mate off his cock. Finn finally let it fall from his mouth with an audible pop.

"I need to get you home," Luke said, working to keep the snarl from his voice. He wasn't mad, but it wasn't like his mate's efforts weren't affecting him. How the hell was he supposed to get his writhing mate out of the pub and, more importantly past a group of shifters without a confrontation?

Not for the first time, Luke wished he'd been a little more attentive when the subject of discussion had been on mates as a teen. He knew next to nothing, but even Luke knew this had to be a special case. If it wasn't special, then it simply wasn't spoken of much because Luke had never heard of it.

He might have stuck around, despite his father's protest and fought for his place as pack leader if it meant being able to protect a future mate more securely. But no, he had thought that path was taken from him by his orientation, and now he was stuck in a bathroom. Luke needed to get Finn home safely where he could have a moment to think with a clear head and breathe air that wasn't laced with his mate's come-fuck-me-pheromones.

Finn stayed relatively still in his arms and Luke thought, grimly, that it had something to do with the short blow job. Perhaps it had sated Finn's uncontrollable desire somewhat, or at least, taken the edge off. He was able to stand now on his own, which meant he could walk.

Luke got an idea that came straight out of every bad spy movie he'd ever seen. He moved the trash can so he could open the door a crack.

"Christian," he hollered. Christian scurried over to the door.

"Is he okay? Something is very wrong, man."

"Yeah, I know. I think he is having a bad reaction, probably shouldn't have mixed alcohol with the meds." Luke hoped Finn wouldn't be too upset by that little fib.

"That looks like more than a bad reaction," Christian said suspiciously.

"Let's just agree there is something serious going on here, alright? Will you help me get him out?"

"Do you need help carrying him?" He was clearly confused.

"I need you to strip," Luke said. "I need your clothes," he clarified after seeing that it was needed. Looking at Christian's expression, he saw his clarification hadn't helped much.

"I'm not getting naked in the back of a pub!" he squeaked.

Luke grimaced. He didn't think his animal instincts would let another male in the same space as his mate while he was so vulnerable.

"Finn, baby, I need you to get in the stall and strip."

Finn complied too quickly for Luke's liking. He was

enthusiastically undoing his pants when Luke shut the door on him and brought Christian in.

"Face the urinal," he ordered Christian. "I'll turn away and just throw them on my shoulder." Luke acted as the middleman, handing Christian Finn's clothes as the pieces dropped to the floor and gathering Christian's clothes. When Christian was changed, Luke leaned in and sniffed him.

It might work if they moved fast. Dressed in Finn's clothes, with the jacket hood up and his head down, the shifters should only be able to smell the mating heat from far away. If he ran.

Even if a curious shifter caught him, once they got a real sniff of him, they would lose interest.

Still, this was his mate's self-proclaimed only friend.

"You are doing me a huge favor," Luke began. Christian cut him off.

"I'm not doing it for you. I'm doing it for Finn. He is a great guy who deserves—well just be what he deserves, got it?"

Luke didn't expect to have this conversation now. "I am what he needs," he said without shame.

"Is this going to be dangerous?" Christian asked, finally pondering his own safety.

Luke could see why Finn had connected with Chris; he was selfless. Luke grabbed the small switchblade he carried. He didn't use it for protection, but if Christian was cornered by a shifter whose nose was too clouded with pheromone to notice he'd gotten the wrong end, then a quick stab would sober him up. He handed it to Christian, but he held it like he'd been handed a turd covered rattler.

"Some people might chase you," he said, giving Christian the honest truth. "Just run to a public area in the opposite direction of Finn's house. Do you know where he lives?"

Christian blushed, Luke scowled. "Yeah, I-I looked it up online the other day."

Normally, Luke would've taken offense to this guy sniffing up on his mate, but since he was literally in the middle of saving him, he would let it slide.

"Gotta go now before his smell wears off." That last statement had Christian's eyebrows shooting up. He'd have questions for sure. "Text when you are safe, but uh, don't come by until..." *Until Finn doesn't want to fuck everything with a penis.*

"Got it, be careful," Christian said, determined.

"You...too..." Luke replied awkwardly. Christian left, and Luke went to his naked mate.

"Hey," he said softly. Finn stood in the middle of the stall in his boxers and looked sort of like himself. Maybe the mating heat was waning?

"I don't feel right," Finn said, his hand idly stroking his cock through the boxers.

"We need to talk about this, but first, I have to get you home. Put these on and then we are going to have to go quick, do you understand?"

Finn gathered his bottom lip between his teeth and sucked on it. He was staring at Luke's crotch but nodded.

Moments later, Finn was dressed and latched to Luke's side. This would work, they looked like a regular couple, almost. Luke held him by his side, guiding him out of the bathroom and through the pub. The tables across the street were empty. Christian had done his job. He kept them at a pace somewhere between a jog and a fast walk until he was able to set Finn on his bike before sliding in front.

The noise his mate made when Luke started the engine

was unbearably erotic. They weren't completely safe yet. Luke ignored the way Finn clutched and rubbed his body and urged his bike quickly down the street. He ignored most traffic laws as he drove and soon, he pulled into Frannie's driveway. He helped Finn off the back of the bike. The drive seemed to have helped him. His legs were steadier. Luke filed all this information away to think on later when his mate was safe.

From across the yard a man, Luke decided it had to be the pack master, stepped forward, standing between them and the door.

"I've seen that movie too," he said smoothly.

Luke didn't know how he'd gotten here so fast. No one had been following him.

Finn looked up at him. "Fuckmesohard," he mumbled.

Luke growled and tightened his hold on his mate.

The pack leader looked shocked for a split second. Then, he was just amused. He craned forward, inhaling the air in front of him. "It's stronger now. In front of the library, it was just the faintest hint of a scent. But it's fading from what it was, even now." He looked at Finn with a gaze that made Luke want to shield him. "Is there a better scent? When my sweet angel went into heat, I would lock her up and tie her down so that I could visit her and bathe in her glory."

"You have a mate?" Luke asked.

"Had," the pack master said packing a million emotions into the one word, pain, love, happiness, insanity. He took a deep breath, shuddering. "You're Luke," he stated. "Your father is a strong shifter. My name is Lucian. What do you think, Luke? Do you think it would work?" Lucian pondered, taking a step toward them.

Luke snarled, it almost sounded like a bark.

Lucian stopped, his eyes narrowed. "Careful, lone wolf. You are in my territory."

"That's right, I'm not a part of your pack, and neither is he, so if you'll move out of the way we can go on," Luke said barely able to hold in all the violent things he wanted to do. Even without Finn by his side, he would've been on edge around the other alpha. Alphas didn't mesh.

"You aren't a part of my pack, no. But him," he gestured to Finn, "he is a novelty discovered in *my* territory. Wouldn't that be something to see? Maybe I'll simply rip him from you and see if I can't fuck a litter into him."

He heard the gun cocking before he saw her. Frannie had slunk out of nowhere. Her curly hair was a mess on her head, and she was wearing her favorite polar bear pajama pants and slippers, an altogether cute look, ruined by the pistol she had pointed at the pack leader's head.

"How 'bout you get the hell off my property and stay the fuck away from my brother."

Bless her, her voice hardly shook.

The pack leader raised a single eyebrow. He wasn't used to being challenged by a woman, especially not a non-shifter woman. He took a step toward her. Luke's gut tightened. How could he protect them both? Frannie leveled the gun and fired. The bullet lodged into her yard right next to the pack leader's foot causing a tuft of grass to go flying.

"My aim isn't great, but it improves the closer you come."

Luke saw her hand shaking. Finn was now trying to push from him to get to his sister.

"The cops are going to be here any minute," Finn said, sounding clear-headed. "You should just leave while you can."

The pack leader appraised him. True enough, sirens

began wailing softly in the background. He bowed his head slightly in mock submission. "Whatever *you* say." He turned in the other direction.

Frannie wheeled on them. "Get in the house, now," she said with much less conviction than she'd had moments before. Her lip trembled, most likely the adrenaline. Finn went to her. Luke wasn't sure who was holding who up. Frannie wrapped a protective arm around Finn and shot Luke a glare that spoke volumes. He waited, not entirely sure if he was welcome inside anymore. Frannie shook her head, "I said get inside, Luke."

Luke obeyed.

CHAPTER NINE

WHEN FINN WOKE UP, he was aware of two very important things. One, he wasn't alone. That was evident from the foot that pressed rudely up against his backside. Second, he was starving. Like, doubled over in pain, he'd eat anything hungry. He rolled over, and Frannie was there, curled on the other edge of the bed. One of her legs was stretched out, and that foot had been the one he'd felt. He tickled that foot and Frannie opened her eyes, wide at first in panic. Then, as she realized she was safe, they narrowed back into a sleepy gaze.

Finn hated that first burst of fear he saw in his little sister's eyes. Hated himself for it.

He couldn't remember much after they'd gotten inside the house. He did remember his little sister standing in front of her own house, trembling as she leveled a gun at that guy. He thought back to before that happened, the confusing walk home, the haze of the pub, Christian...*Oh god, what had he—*

"I know this expression," Frannie said. "The events of

the night before crashed upon him with stark clarity," she said like it was a line from one of her books. It probably was.

"Where's Luke?" Finn asked sitting up while trying not to clutch his empty stomach.

"Probably sitting on the other side of your door listening to every word. I told him he could sleep, that I would watch over you, but he set up camp outside your door like a soldier. A soldier who is still on my shit list!" She said the last part loudly toward the closed door.

"When did you get a gun, Frannie?" Finn asked his little sister quietly while pushing a lock of hair back off of her forehead. It flopped right back where it had been once he moved his hand.

She shrugged. "Before you and Luke, I was alone a lot. Seemed like a good idea. And after yesterday, I'll thank the fates every day that I did have one. That guy was..." she shuddered. "Like kind of sexy but not at all sexy, ya know?"

Finn opened his mouth to answer, but Luke chose that moment to knock. "Come in," Frannie said even though it was Finn's room.

"I-uh..." he cleared his throat and kept his gaze down. "I thought I should go get some food. No one ate last night, and I think Finn will be especially hungry. After..."

"You sneaky fox," Frannie said, effectively covering any awkwardness anyone would feel by Luke finishing his sentence. "I understand completely. My shit list is indeed, an uncomfortable place to be. Go, bring back pancakes. And sausage." Finn knew his sister well enough to tell she wasn't even mad at Luke anymore.

When they were alone again, Finn lay back. "Oh god," he groaned, pulling a pillow over his face. "I made a huge fool of myself last night, Frannie."

She tugged on the corner of her lip. "You did seem really out of it."

"I was possessed. I don't know what came over me. And Christian, I don't even know where he went. And Luke won't even look at me."

"Luke is crazy about you."

He looked out at her from under his pillow. "Speaking of Luke and things that are crazy..."

"Oh, the wolf thing?"

"Yeah, the wolf thing."

Frannie did her best to tell Finn where she met Luke and what she knew about what he was. Having it spelled out to him in no uncertain terms blew Finn's mind. This type of thing didn't exist in his world...and now it did.

"...I mean, you can rebel and rebel against the notion of shifters, but scientists are discovering new species of animals all the time. And you are always hearing about tribes of people who had lived cut off from the rest of the world discovered in the middle of the jungle. It isn't that big of a stretch to think maybe some people also turn into animals. Remember my hamster?"

"Enrique?"

"Yeah, now that I think about it, he was probably a shifter. That's why I was always getting blamed whenever Mom was missing a twenty."

"You were always getting blamed because you were always the one who took her money."

She waved her hands dismissively. "Semantics." She froze like she'd gotten a really good idea. "I bet Enrique and Felix were in on it!"

Their older brother was the apple of their parents' eyes. Their mom did a good job hiding it, but their father gave up trying a long time ago. It was very clear that none of them had measured up to their first born.

Frannie left then for Finn to get dressed. The second she closed the door he wished he could bring her back inside. She was good at keeping Finn's darker side from rearing its ugly head. Now, it was his only companion.

This specific flavor of shame wasn't new. Every time Finn had woken up from a reckless bender in college, naked, most times alone, he had felt this way. Ashamed, embarrassed, and empty. Only now he got to add starving and ragged to the list. His body felt like it had been wrung out like a wet dishcloth.

He stepped out of bed and pulled on a pair of jeans and a t-shirt. He searched for his phone, found it in his jeans pocket, but it was dead. After rummaging around for his charger, he felt a sharp pang of pain slice through his stomach. He needed food badly. It hit him then, the delicious scent of pancakes and sausage. He practically sprinted from his room, but the kitchen and dining room were empty.

"Frannie? I thought I smelled—" Just then he heard the front door open. Luke stepped through, his arms lined with bags of to-go boxes.

"Hey," he said, his eyes downcast.

"About yesterday," Finn began, a pit of hunger and despair gnawing at his stomach, "I'm sorry. I—"

"Please don't apologize," Luke said walking right past him.

He set the food out and grabbed plates, cups, and silverware. When the table was set up, Frannie appeared from the hallway looking showered and ready for the day. "You have returned to my good graces," she said, sitting down at an empty plate and diving right into the Styrofoam boxes. "I forgot, Finners, this came for you." She set an envelope down on the table next to his charging cell phone.

He didn't look at it before sitting down and piling his plate high. His hunger pains were so bad he felt sick. He started eating. More like shoveling the food into his mouth and had gotten three pancakes down before looking up to see Frannie staring.

"Want some juice before you start choking?" Frannie asked. Luke was still looking away from him, and it was driving Finn crazy.

He got it. Finn had made a fool of himself, and if it weren't for Frannie, Luke would probably be gone already. Finn accepted the juice that Frannie had poured. He shoved a sausage link in his mouth and then looked down at the phone. It had charged enough to turn back on. There was a text message from Christian that he quickly opened.

Hey man, I, uh, am not going to be around for a while. Don't worry or anything. I'll text ya when I get back into town.

Finn read the text again. He felt the pancakes turn into bricks in his stomach. He clenched his fingers around the knife and fork in his hands. His gaze fell to the envelope Frannie had set on the table. It was from the university. Trying to look casual, he opened the envelope and pulled out a single sheet of paper. The letterhead stated it was from the Graduate school of Psychology dated one day prior.

Dear Mr. Feller,

The Graduate School of Psychology has received your appeal to re-enter your studies. We appreciate your desire to continue your education but feel, at this time, you would not be a good fit for the current program. We thank you for your interest and encourage you to re-apply with the graduating seniors during next year's application period.

Sincerely,

Robert Paterson Ph.D

Finn closed his eyes. When it rains...He guessed Professor Paterson had had enough time to send out Finn's rejection letter before taking his leave of absence.

His body shook, still feeling achingly empty despite the piles of pancakes he'd shoved down his gullet. He slammed his silverware down on the table. Frannie jumped, and Luke finally looked up at him. It was what was in Luke's face though that was the final straw. He saw it fill his eyes.

Regret.

"Don't fucking look at me like that," he snapped.

Luke winced and set down his silverware slowly.

"Finners, is it bad news?" Frannie asked with a squeaky voice.

He hated that he was the reason her voice was timid. He hated that he'd scared his one friend away and that he was such a fuck-up that the university had preemptively rejected him. He hated the gnawing ache in his gut and his itchy skin. And most of all hated that Mister I Always Want to Know What You Are Thinking had lived through *one* messed up night and had clearly decided that Finn was not what he was looking for after all.

The worst thing? He couldn't blame any of them, not his sister for sensing and fearing his crazy, not his friend for seeing through his pretenses, not the university for not wanting to get involved and not Luke for *finally* seeing what Finn knew the whole time, that he wasn't worth the trouble.

"No, I'm fine, I just...can't do this." It was a little dramatic. He knew that. Finn stood from the table and mumbled something about a shower to the two of them. He stomped down the hallway and into the bathroom, slamming the door and feeling like a fucking child the entire way. He was throwing a tantrum. A twenty-five year old grown-ass man was throwing a tantrum because life wasn't going his way. And when was it?

He turned to the bathroom mirror. Only then did he notice he still held his knife and fork. *Jesus, I am losing it.* He went to the shower and yanked the knob, turning it on hot, full blast. The water shot from the shower head and quickly turned scalding. Without bothering to go slowly, allowing his body time to acclimate to the temperature, Finn jumped in. He gritted his teeth at the hot sprays that hit his sensitive skin like a thousand needles shoving through him.

He'd exited the institution with a single game plan. He'd held onto that like it was his lifeline to humanity, to people. That plan was gone now.

In its place were a thousand doubts and regrets. Next to those were about two million questions. Objectively, he knew stuff was happening to his body and surroundings that didn't make sense with his preconceived notion of what the world was.

He couldn't help but feel it was all because of him, his fault. His karma? Whatever the fuck it all was, it lingered over his head like a cloud of steam, suffocating. Or was that because of the shower? Finn leaned over so that his forehead rested against the wall of the shower just under the spray. He braced himself with his palms, flat on the white siding and took a deep breath, fighting to calm his hyperactive breathing. He knew his mouth was moving. That he was saying something. But as disconnected as he was, he didn't know what it was until he concentrated.

I am worthy. I am worthy. I am worthy. I am worthy.

CHAPTER TEN

LUKE STARED at the piece of paper on the table. His mate had been agitated before, but whatever was written on that page had really ratcheted up his confusion.

And then, Finn had caught a glimpse of the torture going on in Luke's head. He felt like such a dick.

"Luke?" Frannie said only his name, but he heard the questions behind it.

He couldn't tell her what he'd learned the night before. He'd spent the whole night awake, listening for any intruders, but he'd also been on her laptop looking up mating information like a teenaged boy searching for porn. He'd found information. None of it gave him the warm and fuzzies. That was fine with him since his mate wasn't experiencing any warm and fuzzies either. He knew exactly what his mate felt. He could smell it now—a new skill that had sharpened overnight. His sadness and panic were like a bitter berry. It clawed at Luke's nose and throat. If this was how it smelled, Luke couldn't imagine how it felt.

"He's my mate, Frannie," Luke said finally.

She only nodded like he was saying something everyone knew.

"And his body is changing now, to complement mine."

The wheels in her head were turning. Dots were connecting. Her eyes flashed open. "What that asshole said last night, about taking Finn and—is something like that even possible?"

"He won't get to him, but maybe. I'm looking into it. Fuck, Frannie, I've lived on my own for near twenty years, absolutely outside the shifter population. I don't know so much. But it might be possible if Finn's body has adjusted enough."

"And what happened last night? Was that some sort of mating cycle?"

Frannie had figured out in seconds what it took Luke hours to put together. "The effects were worsened by the alcohol Finn drank. It acted as a catalyst, cranking up his symptoms into overdrive."

"But then when it started to wear off..." Her eyes narrowed. "Did you know this would happen? Before you and Finn...did your thing, did you know that this could happen? Don't fucking lie to me, Luke. I don't need a Glock to make you disappear."

He didn't like how she was implying that what was happening to Finn and Luke was somehow a bad thing. It had blindsided Luke for sure, but the reason for it was a good thing. This changed everything in his mind. Once he was sure Finn would be safe, he could begin to finally think about how his entire future had picked up from the path it was on and shifted over like a cartoon road with legs.

Once this was all sorted, Luke could see a different type of future for him and it sure as hell included Finn. "I didn't know," he bit out finally, his voice as terse as it ever had been while speaking to his curly-haired pal.

"You can blow yourself if you think I don't like the idea of what is happening. I'm over the moon about this option opening up for you. It is the person, Luke. My Finn—" she rolled her eyes at his territorial expression. "*Our* Finn is a hard nut, wrapped in a really soft shell. I don't like the stress this is putting on him. Especially after..." she waved her hand in the air in a circular motion, like she was casting a spell that would finish her sentence.

She didn't need to.

The truth was Luke felt like the shittiest shithead in Shit Town. He hadn't been able to look at Finn all morning. Not because he didn't want to but because he couldn't look at him without *wanting* him. The smell of Finn's need wasn't as strong as it had been in that bathroom at the pub. It wasn't gone. Not by a long shot. It had tantalized him all night long, knowing that Finn was on the other side of the door, in bed. At times it had only been the presence of Frannie that had stopped him.

That made him a horrible person. Finn was suffering, and all Luke could think about was fucking him silly. But he couldn't, not until he knew Finn would be safe.

Frannie started clearing the table, boxing the uneaten portions up and stacking dishes. Luke looked back at Finn's spot. The letter was still there. He had an idea of what it meant. His plate still had half a pancake.

The hair on Luke's neck rose. His inner wolf growled. "*I just...can't do this.*" That's what Finn had said before leaving the table. Now, the knife was gone from where he'd been sitting.

Luke jumped to his feet and ran to the bathroom. Fear clouded his mind. He thought back to Finn's scar and opened the bathroom door, using his shifter strength to break the cheap bathroom lock. He stepped inside, disorientated at first by a blast of steam. It cleared, and Luke saw his mate, bent over like he was in pain. He couldn't smell any blood and hoped he wasn't too late.

Luke took a step forward and then heard what his mate was saying. Mumbling over and over, like a prayer.

"I am worthy, I am worthy, I am worthy." Finn shuddered as he spoke, his entire body clenching with stress and pain.

Yes, his Finn was in pain. Luke could no longer allow it.

He stripped and stepped inside the shower, wrapping his arms around Finn. His skin felt overheated. Finn startled and then his body melted into Luke's. He moaned like an addict getting his next fix. The hormones raging inside of him probably made it feel that way. Luke's own body sang with pleasure. His wolf howled with joy. He was back where he belonged, naked with his mate.

"What are you—" Finn said but Luke gripped his chin and pulled his face around so that he could kiss him, silencing him. He speared his tongue through Finn's lips, lapping at his flavor, exploring and tantalizing his mouth. He thrust his tongue in and out, simulating what he wanted to do with his cock. Finn whimpered against him.

"I've wanted to do this since I stopped fucking you a week ago."

"What?" Finn was confused, it showed in his tone, but his lust was growing exponentially. Luke felt it swelling and pouring from his body. He liked the idea that he made his mate so horny he could hardly think. That would be just fine with him, keep Finn well fucked so that he didn't have a chance to think about anything that made him sad or worried. *Not yet, slow down. Make sure it is safe.*

"It has been torture for me, Finn. Not touching you," he slid his fingers down the length of Finn's naked body. "Not tasting you." He licked his neck. "Not reaching out to take what's *mine*." He reached around Finn's tight body and wrapped his firm fingers around his mate's hard length. "Please don't keep it from me again," he murmured against Finn's ear while lightly stroking his cock.

"O-okay," Finn said, trembling despite the warm water pouring over both of them. He kept his face away when he said, "I thought you were tired of me."

"How the hell could you think that?"

"Because...I'm me," he finished sadly and it nearly broke Luke's heart in two. He *was* a shithead if he hadn't done everything in his power to make Finn realize how special, how motherfucking precious, he was to him.

He turned his mate around so that he faced him. He kissed his lips hastily when what he wanted was to take his time. He kissed his chin, his cheeks, covering his face with his lips. "You're right, you are you, and that is what I want. What's happening, to you, to your body, it's scaring the shit out of me, but it doesn't make me want you less. We need to be careful though. I can't risk putting you in a position that would endanger you. I wanted to go slow with you. Romance your socks off."

Finn put a hand against his chest, not pushing him away, but more like steadying himself. "You are you, but you are mine. I hope you're okay with that because it isn't going to change. Not ever." He grabbed Finn's wet hair and pulled his head back, his mouth opened as if by reflex. "Understand me?"

Finn couldn't nod, Luke had too tight a hold on his hair. He said he understood with his eyes though and with the way his tongue flitted out to moisten his lips. His eyes were dark with desire. It was as much as Luke could bear.

He turned his mate around again, slapping his hands against the shower wall with a loud smack. "Stay," he ordered, sliding down on his knees, reverently cupping Finn's ass. He kissed all the skin he could reach while dancing his fingers up Finn's thighs, teasing his balls and the sensitive space just below.

Finn mewled like a sexy kitten. Luke had never been a cat person before, but for Finn, he would make every exception. He spread Finn's cheeks without any warning and thrust his tongue into his hole. Finn howled, and Luke did it again, wrapping his arm around Finn's legs to offer some support for his buckling knees.

"Keep your hands up," Luke growled like a bastard.

Finn whimpered and straightened his legs, but his body was shaking, overcome by sensation.

Luke was merciless with his tongue as he made love to Finn's ass. He wanted to brand him, to make damn sure he would never forget how Luke made him feel, how he would always make him feel. If his Finn wasn't absolutely sure of Luke's desire for him, then it could spell disaster later on. Luke couldn't function with that threat over his head. Finn needed to know without a shadow of a doubt that he was Luke's and always would be. So Luke built the fires of lust, knowing Finn was as hard as he was, would be dripping as he was. But he wouldn't let either of them find release, not until the fire burned away any doubt.

Finn groaned in frustration. He tried to reach down and stroke himself. Luke batted his hand away, and Finn slammed it back against the shower wall. "Please, Luke, I need."

"I know, baby." He delivered a short machine gun blast of tongue thrusts in his tight hole.

"You're making—oh fuck." He tensed and turned, a single shot of liquid flew from his cock, a mini-orgasm that splashed across Luke's face. Finn's eyes widened.

Luke dragged his finger through the hot line on his face and then drew the finger into his mouth, suckling the salty treat. He stood slowly, staring at Finn the entire time. When he stood before him, Luke felt strong and dominant. Nothing in this world could take his mate from him, not while he still lived. "Clean it off," he commanded.

Finn reached for a washcloth. Luke took it from him.

"Nope." He let the p sound pop from his mouth.

The moment Finn realized what he meant, his pupils widened. The idea made him hotter. Of course, it would. His mate was perfect for him in every way. Finn leaned forward and tentatively licked Luke's cheek where the majority of the semen had landed. He moaned. Luke didn't know if he enjoyed the taste or the carnality of the act. He enthusiastically licked Luke's face clean and then leaned back, surveying his good work but with a slightly dissatisfied expression.

"What is it, Finn?" Luke murmured, cupping his face.

Finn stuck his bottom lip out in an adorable pout. "Yours tastes better."

Luke chuckled. "Who am I to deny you?" He guided Finn to his knees. The sight of his lithe body, on his knees, his muscles straining and stretching to rise to the treat Luke was offering him. It almost had him blowing his load right then and there.

Then he wrapped his lips around him and drew him deep in his mouth, and Luke really did almost lose it. Finn's mouth was like heaven. He made tiny noises in the back of his throat that Luke could hear as well as feel. Luke felt his penis bottom out and hit the back of Finn's throat. His balls brushed against Finn's chin, and Luke didn't dare breathe, afraid that the slightest sensation would set him off. Finn offered no mercy though. He cupped Luke's sack, manipulating his most sensitive parts. Then, he flexed his tongue flat under Luke's dick so that each thrust in and out of his sweet mouth dragged over his wet, hot tongue. It was too much.

"I'm going to—"

Finn's mouth became a vise on his dick and Luke felt his explosion begin in bursts of utter pleasure. He held onto Finn's face as he delivered wave after wave of bliss into his mate's waiting mouth. In response, Finn kept his lips latched around Luke. His neck muscles convulsed as he consumed all that Luke had to offer until he finally let Luke's cock slip free while licking his own lips.

"So much better," Finn said a few moments later as Luke helped him to his feet.

Luke grabbed the soap and did a quick wash over of them both. "I don't agree," he said absently, still riding the high of a perfect orgasm. "Mine is different. It's..." Was he about to address himself as a shifter for the first time?

"Dog person?" Finn offered. Clearly, he was trying to be helpful.

"Dog person?" Luke repeated slowly. "I think you mean, lone wolf. Shifter." He turned off the shower and reached for the door.

"Shifter," he said like he was trying the word out on his tongue. "Is that why I'm feeling...different?"

Luke kept his gaze. "Yes. Our sex together, it changed you. Is changing you." Luke stepped out, followed by Finn. His gaze fell on the knife on the counter. He caught his breath. That had been the fear that had driven him in there, and he'd been too distracted to confront it. "Finn, you are quickly becoming my entire life. I need you to know that hurting yourself is no longer an option. Do you understand? If you need to...if, you feel like you might...come to me. Or to a professional. But, no matter what happens, you may not hurt yourself."

Finn's eyes widened. "We already talked about this. Why are you...?" he followed Luke's line of sight, his own falling on the knife that was on the counter. "Oh."

Luke gathered him up, needing him close. "Before you, I wandered in and out of society, never thinking for a moment I could belong. I thought my hopes of a pack were lost that day I came out. But I've found in you and Frannie something I won't willingly let go of. I'll protect it even if it means having unpopular—"

"I didn't even realize I'd brought it. I didn't mean to. I mean, I didn't have any intention," Finn said quickly like he was trying to reassure Luke.

Luke studied him. His breathing was even, his heart steady. He didn't seem to be lying. "You are too special to me, Finn." His wolf could only agree. For the first time in a long time, Luke realized he had something that would hurt like hell to lose. Losing his spot in his first pack had been painful, but losing Finn, his mate was unimaginable.

CHAPTER ELEVEN

"I can take night watch," Frannie said, pulling a steaming aluminum tray out of the oven. Finn scratched the back of his head. "I don't like this, Frannie, I don't like you being in danger."

"Same to you, buddy."

Finn looked to Luke, attempting to give him a, help me out here, look. It was unneeded. Luke's jaw was tense, and he flipped a bottle cap from finger to finger—an agitated gesture that Finn was just learning to recognize.

If he leaned forward and listened, Finn would be able to hear very low and quiet rumblings coming from Luke's chest. Like, he was growling without noticing. Under a different circumstance, it would be hot as hell. Right now, it meant that he was agitated. "Neither of you should be taking watch or being in danger. I can protect you. Both of you."

It was obvious that this was important to Luke. But Finn thought he could forget that idea right away. If there was a fight in their future, he would be beside Luke, not cowering behind him. Frannie, on the other hand, was too caring, too accepting to be placed in a position of danger.

"You can both suck it," caring Frannie said, looking at them. "What are we even up against? That ass is the...leader...?"

"Pack master," Luke replied. "Said his name was Lucian."

"So he obviously has the power of the pack behind him."

"He leads the shifters in this area, so yeah, he can pretty much order them to do what he wants."

"And he wants me?" Finn asked.

"Seems that way."

Finn sat back, letting the information absorb. The idea that he could give life to something, not in the way men had been doing it for years but to actually let it grow inside of him, protecting it, providing for it. His heart warmed. All of his life, Finn was never sure of his purpose or his place. Could this be it? To be a father? There were still a lot of unanswered questions and even with a normal female pregnancy, disastrous things could happen to woman and baby. They needed to be careful.

The table rumbled, breaking Finn from his thoughts. It wasn't the table, he realized, but Luke that rumbled. His nails had lengthened to a point, resembling claws. Finn thought he saw fangs in his mouth before he pushed back from the table, quickly but quietly, stalking away from the table toward the front room and front door. Finn's mouth dropped open. Other than that first time, he'd never seen Luke's shifter qualities manifest. The sane part of him told him it should've frightened him, but it didn't. It intrigued him. He wanted to run his fingers over Luke's claws and feel their curve. Right now though, Luke was peeking out the window, obviously upset by something Finn guessed his human senses hadn't alerted him to yet.

Frannie moved beside Finn, the pistol in her hand again. The safety was off.

"Frannie, give me that," Finn said, reaching for and missing the gun. She grabbed his other hand and crept to join Luke.

"What is—"

A knock at the door cut her off. Luke was the first there, opening it slowly. "What do you want?" he demanded.

Finn strained to hear whoever responded.

"You got yourself into it now, boy," a rough voice like sandpaper replied.

"And you are the first wave? He sends in the old ones first?"

"Could still whip you, boy."

There was something familiar about how they talked, not like normal shit talking between rivals.

"Who is it?" Finn asked, stepping forward. Luke threw a halting hand back, keeping him from whoever was at the door. "Luke—" Finn began.

"Lucian wants him, son. Not letting me in to say my piece isn't going to change that fact."

"Say what you have to say there," Luke said, his entire body was tight, his every muscle, tensed and ready to act.

Luke was a solid wall in front of them. Finn and Frannie could only strain on their tiptoes or duck down low. They wore matching expressions of frustration and confusion.

"I have a package to deliver, and I was told to deliver it straight to your mate in there. You don't want me to get in trouble do you?"

Luke stilled. "Is that what he called him?"

"Well, no, but my orders are the same." The man with the sandpaper voice put his hand against the door. He leaned in and spoke softer. "You want me to come in and deliver this package. Personally."

Finn knew the man wasn't saying anything very important. He took another step forward so that he could put his hand on Luke's shoulder. "Let him in, Luke. The package is for me after all."

Luke looked like he was waging war in his brain. A part of him wanted to do as his mate requested, but the other part was too worried that the man at the door posed a threat.

"Luke," Finn put his hand on his shoulder.

Luke slammed the door shut then. He hauled the three of them back, ordered Frannie to sit at the kitchen table and to turn the safety off. He pulled Finn down the hallway. "I'll let him in, but, if he tries to do anything, if he seems like he is going to try anything, you need to listen to me," he whispered frantically in the dark hallway. "This goes against every instinct. That man is the cruelest man I know, and I loathe the idea of him being in the same space as you."

Finn kissed him lightly on the lips. "I'm not this breakable thing, Luke. I'm not as strong as you, but I can be strong."

"I know, baby."

Luke left him with Frannie and went back to the door. When he came back to the kitchen, he indicated that Frannie and Finn were to stay on one end of the table while the man was at the other end.

Finn didn't expect to recognize the man with the sandpaper voice, but he did. He'd seen him with the pack outside of the library. He looked grisly and dangerous, but again, Finn was struck with the feeling that he knew that face.

"Finn, Frannie, meet my father, Daryl," Luke said with no small amount of sarcasm.

Frannie gasped.

Finn eyeballed the older man. It was a little soon to be meeting Luke's parents.

"Wait, does that mean your dad is with the enemy?"

"To be fair, we just became the enemy. Luke had no issues with my pack—"

Luke snorted. "It wouldn't have mattered."

"Okay, okay. Enough posturing, enough secrets," Frannie said, cutting in the middle of the crowd with her words and body. "The package? What is it? I don't imagine it is flowers and candy."

"Actually, you are only half wrong. There is candy." His father reached a small rectangular box out to Finn. Luke stepped in and grabbed it from him first. "Protective, ain't he?" he said conspiratorially to Finn.

"Of my mate? Damn right," Luke responded, staring at the small box like it held a bomb.

Finn blushed slightly. So, Luke wasn't the type of guy to dial back his feelings when his family was around. That was nice if not a little awkward. "Is he trying to woo me or something?" Asking the question only made his cheeks burn brighter.

Daryl grimaced. "Something like that. I told you, you didn't want to get on this pack master's radar. He is creative and a lot crazy. I don't know for sure. I've been with this pack since your dear mother died. Lucian was new then. They say he lost his mate."

"He spoke about her," Finn remembered. "His sweet angel."

"Since then, he can be a bit...eccentric. Most times he is normal, bearable. But I have seen him get these bees under his bonnet before, and it never ends well for the other party."

"Can't we just, appeal to the pack or something?" Finn asked, not liking how quickly everything was getting violent.

Daryl stared at him. "How much does he know about shifters?" he asked Luke.

Now Luke grimaced as if he'd been caught doing something wrong. "A little."

Finn thought about what he did know of shifters and realized that the majority of his shifter knowledge was bedroom related. He didn't know anything about the politics of a pack. "I don't know much," he said, daring a glance at Luke who had relaxed enough to give him a pervy smile like the mind-reading bastard he was.

His dad ignored their exchange and moved to sit down at the table. Frannie settled in a chair in the middle of the table, gripping the gun with her hand furthest from him. "I'll give everyone the condensed version. Shifters have some heightened senses, even while in human form. Our sense of smell is one of our most useful senses. For instance I can tell that you all use the same body wash and that this little lass shot that gun recently. But, not all shifters have the same senses nor are our abilities equal. Alphas like my son here are born with more sensitive senses. Though, when it comes to the mating hormone, even I could smell ya. That was what originally brought Lucian to you. You were like a candle, and he was a moth."

Finn sat down on the other side of the table. Luke moved behind him, not before setting the package in the middle of the table like an odd centerpiece. Finn figured Luke didn't even want the box close to him.

"What is your point, Daryl?" Luke asked.

"I'm trying to make sure everyone has the information they need to understand what is in that box. So, Finn, you have a scent that notifies those around you of your state. But, since you've been spending time with Luke, your scent has been transfused with his."

"I smell like Luke?"

"Like peeing on a tree," Frannie said with no small amount of glee.

Finn scowled. "What does this have to do with the package?"

"They are candies infused with Lucian's scent. His... personal scent," Luke's father said.

Luke snarled.

Finn jumped. "I don't get it."

Luke's father was grim when he spoke. "Lucian fights dirty and on a basic wolf level. If you ate the chocolate, you would consume the pack master's scent, repelling the wolf in Luke while making your own body more susceptible to accepting the pack master as a mate."

Finn sat forward, stunned. "That's all it would take? A little change in my scent and he wouldn't want me anymore?"

"It wouldn't have worked. I am in control of my wolf. Not the other way around."

Finn didn't know if Luke was trying to convince him or himself. He took a deep breath. "I need to talk to Luke. Excuse us." He stood but then remembered Frannie. "You won't..." he said, not wanting to finish the question to Luke's father.

"I wouldn't hurt a lass so pretty as your sister," Luke's dad said, sounding fifteen years younger.

Frannie rolled her eyes. "We're fine."

Finn led Luke into his room and shut the door. Luke

eyed him warily. Finn turned from him and faced the window. The curtains were drawn so he couldn't see out. He concentrated on the tiny flower cutouts that lined the bottom of the curtains. "Luke, things are getting serious out there. I just met your father and Frannie has a gun, and now some other guy is trying to make me smell like him," he said this all in a rush and hoped Luke would understand him. "We kind of *just* met, so..." He turned but couldn't look at Luke's face. He wasn't sure what expression would be there waiting for him. But, he had to say this before he wasn't brave enough to get the words out. "I'll get it if you need to cut and run. I'm sure that after a while, this will all wear off and that other pack master won't give two shits about me. I won't be that shiny new toy he can't have, and you can just, go about your life, carefree."

"Is that what you want me to do?" Luke asked with calm, measured words.

"I want you to do what is best for you," Finn said, unable to answer the question outright.

Luke erased the space between them with a quick stride. He cupped Finn's face and pulled his body tight up against his own. "You are what is best for me," Luke said before claiming Finn's mouth. He dipped his tongue inside Finn's mouth like he was posting a flag in newly discovered ground. "I don't care if we just met five seconds ago, because, Finn, I knew then too. I knew the moment I saw you bent over that island that you were my mate. I would've stayed then, and I am staying now. You are mine. Frannie is not only your sister but my friend as well. I will protect and defend what is mine."

"We are a sorry pack," Finn said when he could find his breath. "More than half of us are humans."

"You aren't exactly just a human now, Finn. I don't think we've seen the last of your changes."

"I literally have no idea how to respond to that," Finn said.

"Then kiss me again, and promise me you'll stop trying to send me away because honestly, it just makes me want to rip your clothes off, throw you on the ground and show you just how much I don't want to be away from you."

Finn trembled at the mental images that brought up. He held on to Luke's hips as he kissed him back. Too soon though, they were pulling away, as if they both realized that they weren't alone in the house and an extended absence would be embarrassing at the least.

Finn followed Luke back to the living room. Frannie smirked at the sight of them. "Your fly is down," she said to Luke.

"What? No, it's..." Luke looked down and caught on to Frannie's joke too late.

"You know, Daryl, it will be great having someone else around who isn't always boning my brother."

"That's so inappropriate," Finn said.

At the same time, Luke asked, "What do you mean having someone around?"

Daryl stared at the carpet, embarrassed. "I don't want to cause trouble."

"That is nonsense," Frannie said, standing. "You basically just told us your evil boss' entire plan. What will your pack do to you if you go back? If someone finds out you told us?"

Daryl drew himself up, his chest puffing out slightly. "I can handle myself."

Frannie shook her head. "I'm not saying you can't. But it isn't safe for you there now, is it? Not now that you've helped us. I'm not proposing you stay forever. And the first sign of you bashing anyone's lifestyle and you are out. But until we work this all out and I know you won't be beaten to death and dumped in a ditch, you should stay."

Finn felt a chill when neither Luke's dad or Luke denied that as being a possible outcome. "Of course you can stay," he said. "My sister's home is your home."

"You wouldn't have an issue living here?" Luke asked a little too roughly. "With me? And my mate?" He was being hostile and at first, Finn didn't know why, then he thought back to what little he knew of Luke's father, about how and why he had kicked Luke out of the pack so many years ago.

Finn thought he saw a layer of moisture in the older man's eyes. "People make mistakes, son. That was my biggest." He turned to Frannie, "But I don't have a lot to offer money-wise. I mean, I would be added security and would pull my weight around the house, but, Lucian kept most of our wages. I have a part-time gig at a mechanic shop."

Frannie grabbed his elbow and brought him from the kitchen to the living room, taking a seat on the couch and indicating he should do the same. There was a spiral notebook and a pen on the coffee table. She picked it up and turned to a fresh page. "Don't worry about that. Why don't you just tell me how you and Luke's mother met? Was it terribly romantic?"

Finn smiled. To Frannie, stories were currency, and as long as Luke's dad kept them coming, she wouldn't care a single bit that he stayed.

"But what about the rooms? There isn't an extra," Finn said, immediately feeling selfish.

Frannie didn't even look up at him. She was too busy scribbling whatever Luke's dad had said so far. "Just move in with Luke, or have him move in your room if that makes you feel more comfortable."

Considering all they'd done, the idea of staying in the same room as Luke made Finn feel as nervous and giddy as a teenager. He found Luke's face.

Luke smiled at Finn with a smile that was truly wolfish. "Hey, roomie."

CHAPTER TWELVE

LUKE STEPPED INTO THE BATHROOM. His foot, newly covered in a sock still warm from the dryer, fell on a wet towel that someone had haphazardly thrown on the bathroom floor. Luke cursed under his breath. "Finn!" he hollered.

"What?" Finn yelled back, probably from the living room.

Luke heard the TV blasting a kickboxing workout DVD, "Give me four more and three and two and one and hold!"

"Luke, what?" Finn yelled again, out of breath.

He grabbed the wet towel from the floor and carried it down the hallway. As he suspected, Finn and Frannie had pushed the couches back and were both sweating profusely as a too tanned guy on the TV ordered them to squat low.

"Dude, that's not mine. I haven't showered yet," Finn said, squatting. Luke liked what the position did to the shape of his ass. He'd enjoy it more if he wasn't just a little bit worried. In the week and a half that Daryl had been staying with them, Finn had become a bit of a workout junkie. They all limited their time outside and never went anywhere alone, hence the workout DVD Frannie had ordered them online when it became clear that Finn could not calm down. She did them with him sometimes, but just last night Luke had woken up to no mate in his bed only to find him doing push-ups in the dining room.

Luke hated that there was a problem in his mate's life that he couldn't simply fix either through skill or force. That wasn't exactly true. He could challenge Lucian this very moment but had already sworn to every other person in this house that he wouldn't. He could break a promise to his father and Frannie, though it would pain him to break a promise to the latter. But to Finn? Never. So he was stuck, watching his mate's abs become more defined.

There was *one* thing Luke could do that sometimes helped ease Finn's body and mind.

He passed them, continuing to the laundry room. "It might not be yours now, but it was yesterday. I'm tired of getting my socks wet!" he barked like an asshole. His Finn took the bait.

"What the hell is your problem?" he shouted, rising from the squat and stomping after Luke. He crossed the threshold into the laundry room, and Luke slid the door shut, locking it. "I already told you, that towel isn't—"

Luke grabbed his mate possessively at the back of his neck. His other hand went to his lower back so that his arm could absorb most of the force when Luke shoved him back against the washer, his lips already covering Finn's, silencing anything else he had to say.

Finn responded immediately, gripping Luke's biceps tightly. He pushed up on the tips of his toes giving as good as he got.

Luke wasn't in the mood for a power play though, and

lately, Finn responded best to being used. Luke broke the kiss, both of them breathing hard in the small room. He spun Finn around so that his hands pressed against the washing machine. In one smooth motion, Luke yanked Finn's shorts and briefs down over his hips. They lingered just below his knees, but Luke knew Finn liked it that way, not all the way undressed as if they couldn't wait long enough for him to step out. Which Luke found he couldn't.

He pushed Finn's face down so that his cheek rested against the cool metal of the washing machine lid. He reached in his pocket for the lube Luke now kept on him at all times.

"Noooo," Finn wailed, "Use your cock, please baby, I want to feel it again."

Luke set his lips in a hard line, gathered a dollop of lube and applied it between Finn's sweet cheeks. "You know I can't, Finn. We don't know what it will do, what it could do to your body."

"I want it," Finn moaned, and the sound of it went straight to Luke's cock. The wolf inside of him scratched against the cage Luke had placed him in. The wolf cared for Finn but was willing to take the chance when it came to fucking. Luke was not. He would not do anything to harm Finn, ever.

"I'll give it to you, baby, but safely. Until we know more." He paused long enough to roll a condom down his length and then brought the head of his cock against his mate's tight, welcoming hole. "Relax, love. I've got what you need." He pushed forward, but his crazy mate bucked back. Luke passed through his tight outer ring and was fully seated in his ass. It felt tight and warm and beautiful. Finn made whimpering noises, quieter than he would have made if they were alone. Luke grimaced. He liked his mate wild. He pulled out and thrust back in, setting a frantic, savage pace. Finn met him, thrust for thrust, arching his back, curving his body allowing Luke perfect access.

Soon, he felt his own climax coming. It never took long with Finn. He bent over, gripping Finn's chin so he could turn his face and kiss his lips. Finn licked at his lips and brought his hand up to the back of Luke's head, grabbing hold of his hair and tugging with each thrust. He found Finn's hardened cock with his other hand and stroked it with a firm grasp. He swallowed his moan of pleasure as Finn exploded over his hand just as Luke found his own release. He groaned as he spilled himself inside the latex.

He slipped out of Finn and helped him down, holding him against his body. Finn snuggled against him so sweetly, his head fitting perfectly in that space between his shoulder and neck. He breathed quickly still, but it was slowing into soft, sated moans.

"Will we ever be able to have sex without a barrier again?" he asked softly.

Luke heard the want in his mate's voice. "Of course, but we have to be careful, baby."

"I miss the way you swelled inside me that first time. I swear, I came like fifty times, I was so filled by you."

It was true when he used a condom, his cock never swelled, never knotted his mate. It knew there was no point. "I don't fill you up enough without it?" he asked with a rumble.

Finn giggled very softly. "Of course you do." He sat up, stretching his arms.

Luke tried to hide his scowl. Before, a fuck would keep him calm for the rest of the day, then a few hours, now he'd been able to rest for a whole five minutes. He allowed his wolf to scent his mate, something it had needed to do more and more often lately. Not that Luke's feelings had changed or that the scent had changed, just that the wolf had needed more frequent reassurances that Finn was still his Finn, that no one had swooped in and tried to steal him. He still didn't trust Daryl absolutely and was suspicious that this whole thing had been an act, a way to carry out the initial plan he'd warned them of. But, if that was going to happen, it hadn't yet. Finn was still completely and only his.

But for how long?

They couldn't stay stuck in the house forever. Sooner or later one of them would need to leave alone. Finn was restless, but Frannie had a job to do, one that required her to at least leave the house for supplies, paper, ink cartridges, coffee, liquor.

Finn sat up abruptly. "Is there someone here?" he asked, and then the doorbell rang.

Luke stood, disposing of the condom. He helped his mate get his pants up before yanking up his own. He could smell the newcomer now but he didn't miss how it was Finn who had sensed him first.

FINN HELD Luke's hand out of the laundry room to the front door. There, Frannie stood, standing behind Daryl who looked as near to a wolf with its hair rising down his spine as a human could. Finn noticed how Frannie kept one hand at her back near the gun she kept there, thinking Finn wouldn't notice.

He did notice though. That and so much more. Luke had warned him that his changes were far from over and he'd been right. He hadn't warned him about how restless and distracted he would feel. How could he concentrate on reading when he could hear the neighbor's conversation outside or smell what the lady across the street was making for the man who was not her husband?

Secrets. That word held more meaning to him now. His neighbors kept fewer secrets from him now that he could sense most everything they did. Like how the house across the street smelled like sex two hours after the man of the house left for work. Or how Frannie cried in her room sometimes at night and trembled every time she made herself touch that stupid gun.

Or the way Finn's body felt like it was burning from the inside out.

It had started slowly, a mild discomfort, which had blazed into a raging inferno of pain that he spent every moment trying to hide from Luke. The only time he didn't have to try was when they had sex. And lately, even that hadn't offered as much of a reprieve as it had before.

Luke clenched his fingers, a silent signal to step closer to him. Finn obeyed. It was easier than setting him aside every single time to explain that he was not a fragile doll at constant risk of breaking.

Frannie cleared her throat—it was supposed to be her house after all. "Who is it?" she asked. Finn swelled with pride. Her voice was as clear as a bell and without a single worry. A stark contrast to the perspiration at her forehead.

The four of them waited with bated breath. This was what kept them inside, what forced them to leave the house as a group, not knowing what the pack master had planned. Would he send another messenger? Or would he send something that would put an end to them all and get rid of the problem?

"I-I don't even know who I am asking for," a young male

voice called through the door. "Christian sent me, said I would be safe here."

Finn bit his lip. After that first text from Christian, he hadn't received anything else. He'd assumed Christian had been avoiding him. But there was no malice in the voice on the other side of the door. In fact, the tone clenched at Finn's gut. It was laced with worry and exhaustion. "Let him in," Finn said, though, none of the other three opposed him.

A slender boy entered, no more than twenty. He wore a tight-fitting black t-shirt and jeans and a large bruise that colored nearly his entire face. A cut split his bottom lip, and threads of color spread out from it like the proof of the pain it gave him. "Is one of you Finn?" he asked with a quiet, weary voice.

"I am," Finn said, stepping to stand beside Luke.

The boy gave a look that was exactly halfway between a smile and a sigh. He bent down so that he was on his knees as if he was bowing before a king. Frannie was the first of them to recover and break out of their shocked circle. She knelt beside him, an arm around his shoulders while the other held him loosely around his waist.

"You're okay now. You are where you are safe."

If this was a trap by Lucian, they were all doomed. But every sense in Finn told him that boy was feeling honest emotions. On top of that, he trusted that Luke and Daryl's senses were at least more practiced than his and neither of them seemed on edge by the boy, just bewildered. It made sense—the older was used to the rough life of a pack while the younger had spent half of his life alone.

"Get up, now," Frannie ordered gently. "Let's all go into the kitchen."

The kitchen was the place for important conversations.

Seated and with a cup of chamomile tea, the boy, Sorell, told them about how he'd been a junior pack member in a shifter pack that had formed at his school. His parents had frowned upon the shifter lifestyle and expected Sorell to do the same. When it was clear he could not, they had kicked him out. According to him, that had been the best thing to happen to him until his pack had experienced the corruption that comes from appointing the most power hungry of the pack as leader.

The new pack master had gotten the entire pack into the drug business, going as far as requiring each pack member to use so they would be hooked and bound to the business. Sorell had simply wanted out, and it had almost cost him his life. When the story got to Christian's involvement, Sorell clammed up.

"That is Christian's business to tell," he said with a bit of steel.

Finn figured he could've pushed the issue, but why put Sorell in another tight spot? Bruised and thin, he looked like life hadn't thrown him too many favors.

Frannie was clearly already on board with Finn's train of thought. She had him set up with a second mug of tea and a large slice of angel food cake. She always kept a container around saying it was okay because it was fat-free.

Sorell looked like he didn't quite know what to think of Frannie. It made sense, Finn thought. Frannie probably wasn't anything like the shifter women from his pack. He made a mental note to ask Luke exactly what shifter women were like.

In the end, they decided that Sorell would stay on the couch until they could find a better place for him.

At first, it was a little awkward with Sorell around, but he and Daryl quickly learned they had more in common than anyone expected. Sorell was good with cars, actually, any mechanical thing. He fixed Frannie's juicer, much to Luke's chagrin who had told her the week before that it was junk.

Just when everyone was getting used to Sorell, the doorbell chimed again. Again, they circled around the door, only now with Sorell at Frannie's side as she called out a clear, "Yes? Who is it?"

That was how they met Pippen. He was another transplant from Sorell's old pack. He came with news that things had just gotten worse, that the pack was also getting into the sex trade market. Finn was more relieved than ever that Sorell, and now Pippen, had come to them. No one should have to lead that life who didn't want to.

Pippen was an odd one, not finding his spot quite as quickly as Sorell had. Finn understood that. If it weren't for Luke, he'd probably still not know where he was supposed to be. He was jumpy too. With his fair skin and hair, but dark, dark brown eyes, he reminded Finn of a bird or like one of those fairytale creatures from some animated movie.

When Conner rang the bell, tanned and outdoorsy, saying he'd heard on the road that a new pack was forming that wouldn't expect its members to sell or do anything illegal to belong, they decided it was time for another kitchen meeting.

"This is bad news," Daryl said with his sandpaper voice. "Taking in one old stray wouldn't have mattered much, add another pup and you are mostly still fine. But now we have five shifters in this house. Lucian won't be able to ignore that even if he wanted to. This is his territory. Five of us in this house is pissing on that. Add Finn to the mix, and you're asking for a turf war."

"Leave Finn out of it," Luke growled.

Sorell stood. "We don't need to stay here for long," he said. "The three of us, we could move on."

"And go where?" Frannie asked.

"I don't know, maybe start our own pack," Sorell said.

"Without an alpha?" Daryl said disbelievingly. "Even with an alpha, a pack can go to shit. Without one? You are asking for trouble."

"We could go lone," Pippen said, with his soft voice. "The three of us."

Conner sighed, but his tone was patient. "That isn't lone if we are all together."

Finn wished he had some of Conner's patience. His skin felt prickly and over-sensitized. He paced along the kitchen wall, Luke standing in front of him, swaying slightly with his movements like a magnet.

"Why not just be a pack then?" he asked, a little belligerently. "We have an alpha. We even have a den mother," he tried to add that last bit to soften his gruff delivery.

Frannie scrunched up her nose and narrowed her eyes at him. "I am not a den mother. You obviously mean Daryl." That got the laugh that Finn's joke did not.

Finn wasn't offended. He hadn't been great in social situations before. Now that he had seemingly no control over his libido and his own body was attacking him from the inside out, he was even less equipped to charmingly handle social situations.

"Finn, I'm hardly qualified," Luke mumbled, but the other four shifters were already looking at him differently. Sorell, Conner, and Pippen all looked like they were sizing him up while Daryl's gaze swelled with pride.

"Why aren't you? You are an alpha, and you have a mate," Finn gestured to himself. "You've got that growly thing that makes people do what you say."

"There is so much more to it than that," Luke said, with as much of a raised voice as he ever had toward Finn.

Finn shrugged like he didn't care, but really he felt like he was suffocating. With the extra guests, alone time had been harder to find, so even his quick fixes were coming less often.

Which meant so was he.

He knew it was all biology. That the hormones in his body were building to prepare him for something that would never happen as long as Luke had his way.

Was there a limit? Every day Finn felt like he'd reached his, only to wake up the next day and realize he could take more, that he had to take more. The suffering was hard, but hiding it was becoming near impossible.

The walls felt like they were closing in on him. His workout pants and black t-shirt felt too tight. "I have to get out of here," he said, pulling the neck of his shirt out to allow some fresh air against his skin. He looked up to find every set of eyes staring at him with varying levels of concern and curiosity.

"I know what you mean," Frannie said quickly, opening the kitchen window. "We've all been cooped up here, and while I am used to long stretches of time without real human interaction, we are running low on the basics. Food, toilet paper, coffee, vodka, all important things if I am going to keep my books flowing. Which, are the only reason any of us are even here right now."

Luke backed up so that he stood protectively in front of Finn. It almost annoyed him. What was there to protect him from in that kitchen? The most dangerous person to him was himself. Finn stomped away from the wall to the center of the room. "Let's go shopping," he said with mock enthusiasm.

CHAPTER THIRTEEN

Frannie flashed her member's card to the employee at the large warehouse-style entryway. The elderly woman's smile dropped the moment she caught sight of the remaining six of them. Luke, holding Finn's hand like he was ready to whisk him away at the slightest indication of danger. Daryl and Sorell both looked like they were casing the joint while Pippen's and Conner's wary eyes searched every corner for signs of trouble.

Only Frannie seemed to be oblivious to the scene they were making. On second thought, Finn figured perhaps it had been foolish of them to all go together. It was too late now.

"Okay, round up," Frannie barked like a football coach. "If we go out in pairs and meet back here to load the cart we can get this done quickly. I know none of us really loves it in this huge crowd, with too bright lights, and shitty piped-in music but we all want to wipe our asses, so this needs to get done. Daryl and I will take the fruits and veggies. You three musketeers will take bathroom necessities and, Finn, you and Luke check out the frozen foods. You look like you need to cool off."

Finn wasn't sure she was joking. He was still sweating, no doubt Luke could feel it in his clammy palm. They all nodded and turned toward their respective areas. "Finn," Frannie called, "don't forget my Hot Pockets. Or you're off the island."

"Are you gonna let me in that head of yours?" Luke asked once they'd gone out of earshot of the rest of them.

"On what?"

"What is going on with you. How many times do I need to tell you, I am interested in anything you have to say, or don't say."

Finn pulled his hand free, needing to let it air out a little. When would he stop sweating? "Nothing is going on. I just feel claustrophobic. I'm being smothered."

"Because of me?" Luke challenged.

"No, Jesus, not everything is about you, Luke." Finn rotated to stomp away from him.

Luke grabbed Finn's hand again, halting him on his way to charge forward toward the frozen foods. The rough touch sent a thrill through Finn that shot straight to between his legs. He did not want an erection in front of the frozen juice and novelties section.

"You are causing a scene," Finn hissed between his teeth and pulled his hand free again.

"I don't fucking care, *mate,*" Luke said, yanking Finn back flush against his body. "You are my mate, aren't you?"

This was not the time or place, but Finn could not ignore the dominance that laced Luke's every movement and word. His body responded to it on a level that needed little contribution from his mind. He licked his lips and nodded, quickly. "Yes, I am yours."

Luke crushed his lips with his own, claiming him in front of everyone, in front of the frozen orange juice and any shopper that happened to pass by.

And Finn let him. More than let him, egged him on, did everything short of yanking his own pants down and bending over.

Someone cleared their throat once and then again, a little louder. With a growl, Luke pulled away, most likely to yell at whoever interrupted them.

A little old lady wearing a pink sweater, matching pink lounging pants and glasses that hung around her neck like a necklace, stood a few feet away. She smiled at them sweetly. "I hate to interrupt, but I need some help grabbing a box off the shelf over there. You look strong enough to assist me," she said with a smile to Luke.

"Um," Luke stalled.

"Go on," Finn urged him. "She can't get it on her own. I'll wait right here." Finn leaned back against the freezer door, watching as the old woman took Luke almost to the other end of the aisle, pointing to something on the top shelf.

He looked behind himself and noticed he was right in front of the Hot Pockets. Smirking, he grabbed a few boxes.

"Hey, do I know you?" a man asked.

Finn had been so absorbed by replaying Luke's moment of dominance while clutching a stack of thin boxes that he jumped at the question. The other guy reached out like he was ready for any boxes that were in danger of falling. Finn tried to place him.

He was disarmingly handsome. Like someone you expected to see staring at you from the pages of a cologne ad. He had dirty blond hair and looked up at Finn beneath long, thick lashes with a smoldering gaze. His eyes were a shocking shade of green. Like a forest covered in a light frost.

"No, I don't think so," Finn said, not really reacting to the man more than simply noticing his features. Luke was down at the endcap of the aisle now. The little old lady looked to have enlisted his help for one more thing, maneuvering a box of some paper goods from the very top shelf. The combination of watching Luke's body do manual labor and knowing he was performing a kindness was too sexy.

"Really?" the guy moved so that he stood in front of Finn, obstructing his view. He stepped forward toward Finn and Finn straightened, taking a step back.

He brought a hand up and tapped his chin like he was thinking. Finn noticed his sleeve tattoo, the ink was startlingly dark, like it was brand new.

"Weren't you in my Intro to Counseling? With Paterson?"

Finn blinked.

"That dude is such a dick, am I right?"

Finn had taken that class, with that professor.

But then why didn't he recognize this guy? He'd really must have been self-absorbed. Finn vowed to observe more of his surroundings.

"I always sat in the back," the guy said as if apologizing for Finn's lack of observation. He stepped closer, and Finn backed away again. Poor guy, he was just trying to have a regular conversation from a regular distance, it wasn't his fault that Finn wasn't able to get too close.

"I sat in the back too," Finn said.

"I know," the guy looked at him from under his lashes again, a slight pink to his cheeks. "I used to watch you."

Finn stumbled a few steps. The guy's confession literally caught him off guard. He tried to find Luke but discovered the two of them had wandered out of the frozen food section. They were now on the other side of the main hallway and in the coffee and tea. It smelled great, but Finn didn't like not being able to see Luke. "I'm sorry, I was going through a lot back then. What's your name?"

"Christian," the guy said with an easy smile.

Finn froze. Now that he thought about it, this guy could play Christian in the movie made about his life. Like, he was the Hollywood version of him. But he wasn't Christian. "No you're not," he said before he could stop himself.

Judging by the way the stranger's easy smile fell, he'd assumed Finn would recognize the name as someone from his class and would be even surer that he should know him. This guy clearly didn't know Finn though, hadn't taken that class and most assuredly was not Christian McGannon.

He *was* the guy who had managed to silently separate Finn from his alpha.

"Well," the man smiled again, but this time it was all fangs. "That almost worked." He snagged Finn's wrist in a vise-like grip, forcing him to drop all of his Hot Pocket boxes on the ground.

The place where his palm touched Finn's skin seemed to tingle, not pleasantly, but in an inherently uncomfortable way. Like the feeling of when he used to put his tongue on a nine-volt battery.

"Let me go," he ordered, but at the same time, he fought a swelling feeling of wrongness. Like his body knew this man shouldn't be touching him. Like it was physically rejecting his touch.

"What are you going to do? You're barely upright. I can smell the mating hormone all over you. And something else, raw," he sniffed lewdly, "*painful.* That alpha lets you walk around feeling like that? Must be more sadistic than mine."

One moment, he was struggling alone against the stranger. But within the space of a blink, Finn was flanked by Sorell and Conner as Pippen lingered back behind the man.

The three of them didn't look scared or worried as he'd seen most of them look in the past. At this moment, they were a pack of predators, lean and dangerous, dark and ruthless.

"What is this?" the stranger said, trying to sound bored. Even Finn could tell he hadn't expected any resistance, much less a pack of it. "A pack of pups?"

Sorell flashed him a smile that was all false flirtation. There was a menace that danced behind his eyes, something that hinted to a darkness lurking within his baby blues. "We don't bite," he said, and then Finn noticed the knife he wielded. It wasn't overly large, but it looked sharp, deadly and well-used.

"Lucian know about you three? He'd be interested to hear about a rogue little pack of hooligans running around with *his* mate."

Everything in Finn rebelled at being addressed that way.

"But who will tell him?" Pippen whispered the threat so quietly Finn almost didn't hear the words. He heard the menacing tone though, that was not hard to pick up, especially since it contrasted so starkly against the shifter's higher-pitched, melodic voice. Pippen shifted forward, slipping the tip of his weapon against the man's back.

Finn was amazed. The most aggression he'd ever seen from Pippen was when he dropped his waffle during breakfast once and had softly cursed. Finn didn't know this thin assassin who looked very comfortable about to take a life.

"Pippen," Conner said, "You're upsetting him."

Pippen's gaze flashed to Finn. "Sorry, boss," he said in his usual gentle Pippen tone. "What do you want me to do?"

The little shifter was asking him if he wanted him to commit murder.

He had that in him? More importantly, he thought Finn should make the decision?

"I..." The stranger *had* said that the pack master would be upset to hear about the three of them.

He never has to know...

"Sorell, did you find the soap?" Daryl asked like a clueless bull tripping into a very tense china shop. The stranger used the distraction to step away from Pippen's knife and toward Finn. He grabbed Finn, shoving him toward Sorell who had to move his own knife quickly so as to not stab Finn himself. The whole maneuver took half a second, and the man was nearly out of the store by the next second's end.

"Come on, Grandpa!" Pippen squeaked.

"Who are you calling grandpa?" Daryl asked, still clueless.

Conner bristled as Daryl clenched his hands into fists and jerked toward Pippen.

"Stop." That one word, not even spoken at conversation level, weaved through the five of them. Each shifter froze. Finn was trying not to faint. Luke took in the sight of Pippen and Conner, frowned when he noticed Pippen's knife, frowned deeper when he saw Sorell's. "What happened?"

"Some shifter just tried to kidnap your mate," Conner said slowly but confidently. "We stopped him. But then, your pa literally stumbled in giving him the distraction he needed to get away." He hadn't said it outright, but his intention was clear. Conner didn't one hundred percent trust Daryl.

"I—" Daryl sputtered. "I did what?" He whirled around to where the stranger had sprinted away. It was almost comical.

Finn stopped listening. His ears felt like they were full of bees. His stomach clenched. The stranger had touched more of his skin when he'd shoved him, and it had started a chain reaction inside of Finn's body. First, he'd been light-headed, then his breath had been short, now his skin burned and prickled, feeling like a living thing. An unhappy, writhing thing that didn't want to be touched by anyone else. The wall he'd built to hide what he was really feeling, began to crumble, and once it started, Finn couldn't stop it. He caught Luke's eyes, confusion flashed behind them, then fear. Finn knew his own eyes would be wide with panic. "Help me."

Luke strode forward, brushing past the squabbling pack he reached Finn, pulling him closer to him. The rush of panic and pain coming off his mate was like being hit with a semi-truck. Desperation and need had slammed against Luke with a force that threatened to take his breath away. How was his Finn feeling like that? When had that started and how had he hid it? Those questions were all secondary to his primary mission of taking Finn away from this place of near danger and giving him what he needed, all that he needed.

"Sorell, find Frannie, finish up and go back to the house. No fighting," Luke ordered over his shoulder. He had Finn locked to his side, one arm protectively around his middle as he led him out of the store. He palmed Frannie's car keys.

"How will they get back?" Finn panted.

It squeezed at Luke's heart that Finn could be experiencing so much pain and still worry about his sister and the pack. That was why Finn needed Luke, to worry about him. "They'll manage. How long have you been like this?" He didn't mean to put so much bark behind his question.

"Feels like forever. Weeks? Since that first episode at the pub. It's gotten worse."

"Why did you hide it from me?"

"I didn't want you to worry," he choked the answer out. His face was flushed, perspiration shone over his forehead. He bit his lip, obviously holding back a scream.

He didn't need to scream for Luke to know he was hurting. Luke could smell it now. It choked him, clawed at his neck and throat, made him desperate to stop it. He looked around them. He turned the car down an exit so suddenly the tires squealed. He maneuvered down a short road.

"You're going to the park?" Finn asked like he was in a daze.

"There's an access road down here, usually abandoned. It's where I parked whenever I wanted to shift and hunt in the forest."

"Hunt? Like for squirrels?"

"More like for deer."

Finn made a disgusted face—a mostly pained—disgusted face. "That's gross—ah!" He clutched at his midsection.

"What? What is it?" Luke asked frantically.

"I don't know, my insides feel like they are cramping up, clenching in on each other," he said through gritted teeth.

Luke drove a little farther so that the car was

surrounded by trees on three sides. He stopped just around a corner. "Get out."

Finn's hands fumbled at the seatbelt. Luke was already out of the car and wrenching Finn's door open. His claws distended and he cut the safety band, lifting his mate out of the car. He took him around to the front. There wasn't much time for the preliminaries. The wolf in him knew what needed to be done. It had known the moment he'd first been assaulted by all that his Finn was feeling.

He ripped Finn's loose pants down. He was aroused. Luke stroked him as he pulled his own pants down, bending Finn over the hood of the car. Finn moaned with each stroke. Luke let go so he could spread Finn's cheeks, rubbing the naked head of his cock against Finn's sweet opening. His precum jetted out, splashing against his hole. The noise Finn made was throaty and raw.

"Yes, finally," he moaned like a prayer.

Luke waited only a moment more, a moment for his fluid to help ease Finn, to sensitize his nerve endings so that he would feel only pleasure. Finn bucked his ass back. Luke smiled and then lined up. With one single thrust he entered his mate fully.

He felt like howling, thought for a moment he actually had. Luke forced himself to calm down, to remain in control. He'd kill himself before he let himself hurt Finn.

"No, please, Luke, don't censor yourself," Finn said as if he could feel the hesitance in Luke's withdrawal.

"I can't hurt you," Luke said and it sounded like a beg. "What if I go too deep? Too hard?"

"I was already hurting. This, this is what I need," Finn said, drawing the word *need* out like it was made of many more syllables. He stretched his back, pushing his ass back at the same time, swallowing the space between his puckered hole and Luke's cock.

Luke snarled, the exact noise his wolf wanted to make. He gripped Finn's waist hard, he'd have bruises tomorrow. Luke would kiss them and probably suck him off as an apology but right now, he could only slam forward, burying himself once again to the hilt. He kept a brutal pace, his balls slamming against Finn's cheeks with a beautiful slapping sound. He kept it up as he felt his mate tense and then heard him groan a release. Luke reached down to pump his mate's cock, not because he needed it to orgasm, he'd already done that. Instead, he gathered some of his seed on the tips of his fingers and brought it to his mouth, savoring his flavor, pounding forward even harder and faster.

Then, he pulled out completely, grabbing Finn by the upper arms as he whimpered. He lifted him up and slammed his back against the side of his car as he entered him from the front. Finn latched his legs around Luke's waist and leaned his head back, seemingly content to be plundered.

Luke felt as if he was at his most basic level, hard, buried in his mate. His inner animal, his human side and his mate all in perfect harmony. It was an overwhelming feeling that he would never back away from. He felt his own release build, but unsheathed as he was, he was bound to swell inside of his mate's sweet hole. There was nothing to do now about it though. His vision flashed red as the head of his cock swelled, locking himself in place, ensuring every ounce of his seed would remain inside.

The pleasure was unimaginable. He could do no more than groan and growl as he emptied himself inside of his mate. Finn had begun whimpering. His cock was rock hard between them and he had come again, coating the front of them both with his fluid. He was still hard and moments later, was coming again, soaking them both. Luke lost count of the times his mate tensed and released. He let his body fall so that he was on his back, Finn at his front as they both rode the endless waves of ecstasy.

CHAPTER FOURTEEN

FINN SLOWLY CAME BACK to his senses, the cloud of pure bliss lifted enough for him to remember who he was and where they were. The sun shone high in the sky. Birds cheeped and chirped in the trees around them, probably telling the other birds all about the debauchery they had just been witness too. Finn shifted, amused at the realization that he was still on top of Luke. It didn't seem to bother him. The hard planes of his chest rose and fell with his even breathing. Was he sleeping? Wouldn't that be just like his man?

"I'm not sleeping, mate," Luke rumbled, his eyes still closed. "I'm recovering."

Recovering? Finn cocked his head to the side. He sat up and only then did Luke slide out of him. Finn let out a little giggle. He felt great. Amazing actually. His limbs were loose and limber. He felt sated, complete. There was no annoying buzzing at the base of his skull, no colony of ants skittering across his skin. He could've been disturbed at the idea if he'd really let himself think too hard on it, but why bother when his entire body felt like it was glowing from the inside out? Warm, satisfied.

"Let's never leave," he said and felt Luke's laugh reverberate through his chest.

"Never leave the state park turnoff on milepost twenty-three? You aren't hard to please."

Finn sat up and stretched his arms. "I'm really not," he said, but there was more to his words, more that he had to say to Luke.

Luke pouted. "I'm sorry, Finn. I was terrified, still kind of am, about what this could mean. I didn't know you were hurting so much."

Finn smiled. "And say that you will never keep your sweet love stick away from me again."

Luke's face contorted into a look that conveyed equal parts distaste and amusement. "I will never say 'sweet love stick,'" he replied.

Finn laughed out loud. "For the best."

"But I won't," Luke said, lifting himself up so that he leaned on his elbows. "Keep it from you, I mean." He lunged forward and kissed Finn quickly, chastely, on the lips.

"We should get back," Finn said finally. He was still worried that they'd basically left his friends and family stranded.

Luke groaned and stretched. He held Finn against his body in a tight hug before lifting him up and himself into a standing position. "I guess we should. We left some drama. Want to tell me about the shifter who tried to kidnap you?"

"It was really weird. He tried to pretend like he'd been in my same class in grad school. I only caught him because he was trying to pretend he was Christian. But, I mean, makes sense, I didn't really talk to Christian a lot until after I...until after. If someone was doing the bare minimum on trying to con me, I mean, I don't know." He shrugged. It all seemed like a lot to go through just to take him.

"That little old lady was in on it," Luke said with narrowed eyes.

Finn couldn't catch the laugh that burst from him. "Words I never thought I'd hear you speak."

Luke scowled further. "It would be funny if it weren't your safety we were discussing. If I see that lady again, I will—"

"Help her across the street," Finn said.

Luke grumped. "Good thing the pack found you."

He'd said it offhandedly, but it was the first time Luke had referred to their little motley crew as a pack, out loud anyway.

"That's something I needed to talk to you about," Finn said. "Before you showed up, Sorell and Pippen they were, I almost didn't recognize them. Pippen actually asked me if I wanted him to kill that guy."

Luke didn't seem surprised at all. He found Finn's pants, helping him in them before sliding his own up his hips. They sat at his hips in a way that reminded Finn what they were shielding. His mouth watered. "In the back," Luke said, guiding Finn to the back seats. "I ruined the front seat-belt," Luke said in answer to Finn's questioning look.

Finn flushed. It had been over the top hot at the moment. Now he was stuck in the back like Luke was some sexy chauffeur.

Luke got in and looked at him in the rearview mirror. Finn could only see his eyes but knew he was smiling, probably making his own Driving Miss Daisy jokes. "Those three," he began, his tone sounding all the more parental because of how they sat in the car, "have had a hard life. Conner seems to have been able to avoid a lot of trouble, and you can tell in his mannerisms, but Sorell and Pippen, those two have clearly not had an easy go at life.

"They remind me a little of me actually when I was excommunicated from the pack. Shifters are born from shifter parents. Both of them don't have to be, but one of them does, and that almost always means they live in the confines, some look at it as safety, of a pack. Sorell's case is different, but he still found a pack. The urge is strong in us to congregate, to form bonds with each other. They've lost that, and from the sounds of it, that isn't a bad thing. But now that they believe they've found a new pack, I don't doubt that they would go to almost any length to keep its members safe."

"Have they? Found a pack?"

Luke shifted away from the mirror so that Finn could not see him. Had he been embarrassed that moment before he turned? They were on the highway now, maybe he was just concentrating on the road. "If you agree to it," he said quietly. "I can't—I won't do it without you by my side. And we'd need to find a new house eventually. It isn't fair to Frannie. We could do it right, a pack the way it was always meant to be, no drugs or crime, no restrictions on what members can and can't be. Just, an accepting group of like-minded individuals who look out for each other."

"Led by you."

"Led by *us*. How many times do I have to show you, my future includes you for as long as you will allow it."

Finn thought he might have to show him right now, on the side of the highway. Then, he realized they really needed to get back to the others. Now that he thought about all that had gone on, they'd left them in a bit of a tumultuous situation, and Frannie was completely in the dark. He thought about what Luke was asking him. "I don't know,

Luke. How am I qualified? A little more than a month ago I was being released from an institution. I've had about a million near breakdowns since then. You are a born leader, a born alpha. But me? I still struggle with deciding what shirt to put on in the morning."

Luke shrugged. Finn saw the tops of his shoulders rise from behind the seat. "Then go naked. In fact, that might be my first official alpha decree. All Finns of mine shall at all times be naked and ready for me."

Finn scoffed. "All Finns? You have more than one of us?"

"Nope, just you," he said, grinning.

"I never pegged you for one of those kinky doms, parading me around like a sex slave."

The car jerked, like Luke's foot had fallen on the brake accidentally.

"How do you know about kinky doms?" he asked.

Now Finn grinned, then he rolled his eyes. "Dude, I'm twenty-five. I've seen basically *all* the porn."

The car resumed a safe, normal speed, but Luke wasn't grinning anymore. "And no parades," he grumbled. "You are for me to see. Only me."

A minute later, Luke pulled down the street to Frannie's house. "Does that mean it's official? Do we need a plaque or something?"

"Nope, we just need to go tell the pack," Luke said grimly as he pulled up.

Finn recognized the reason for his tone immediately. Their pack was on the lawn about to tear each other's throats out.

CHAPTER FIFTEEN

Luke hurried out of the car to reach Finn's side. He didn't think there was much danger to his mate in this situation, but there was tension, and his animal demanded he be near his mate in case he needed protecting.

As it was, his father looked to be in the most danger, the way Conner kept eying him, watching and observing the way he shifted his weight. It looked like a predator memorizing the motions of his prey.

The darker part of Luke begged him to stand back, see how far it would go. His father hadn't cared much about how Luke would protect himself from the world twenty years ago. He sighed. It would offend his mate and probably Frannie. She'd grown a little attached to the old man just because he knew how to spin a story.

"I thought I told you to handle this," he said to Sorell who was in the doorway, Frannie behind him. She danced from foot to foot making worried noises.

"I deserve a medal for getting us all this far without transportation. Besides, they got to talk this out, boss. Some valid concerns here."

Luke was afraid of that.

"Maybe we should go to the kitchen," Frannie suggested in a squeaky voice.

Luke ordered them all to the backyard, that way if things got out of hand, hopefully, less of Frannie's things would be broken. Finn sat with Frannie at the patio table, Luke stood beside them. In the yard, Daryl faced off against Conner and Pippen with Sorell neutrally standing between them.

"The more I think of it, the less it makes sense," Conner said, a little bit of an accent coming through, maybe British or Australian? "That guy knew too much to be just some lackey. He had knowledge of Finn. But not the whole story. Almost like someone was sending out intel as quick as they got it without really investigating. And who else has been here from the beginning? I just got here, Pippen arrived a few days ago. We had no idea you existed before that, and until this afternoon I didn't even know Finn had attended grad school for a time. I trust Sorell and think you do too. And who stumbled in, right at the exact moment so that guy could run?"

"Hold on here, I'm being framed for some bullshit. I'm in as much danger as anyone else here, more than the lot of you because I don't have the excuse of just not knowing the territory, I have no ignorance to claim, the opposite. You just got here," he said to Conner. "And then this guy pops up? Seems convenient to me."

"It can seem anything you want it to. I can show you the proof of why I sought out an honest, law-abiding pack." Conner lifted his shirt. Luke caught a glimpse of a horrendous set of scars across his front that seemed to go farther up. "You, however, have just now seemed to see the error of your ways."

"That doesn't change the fact that by living here I've signed my death warrant with my old pack."

"Unless that's all something you've already worked out with your pack master," Pippen said softly from behind Conner.

"My pack master is standing right there," Daryl shouted, pointing at Luke. "My son. Think what you want about me, but do you really think I would betray my son?"

"Again?" Sorell said.

The word silenced them. It sat in the yard like an elephant.

Luke felt his insides prickle. Finn slid a hand inside his own and clenched his fingers tightly, reassuringly. He squeezed back a thank you before releasing his hand and turning on his father. "Have you been spying on us?" Luke listened for any sign that his father might be about to lie. He doubted he was the only one doing it.

Daryl's heartbeat remained steady, his breathing never changed, his pupils stayed constant. "No."

"Do you know how the pack master might have had so much information about Finn?"

This time his gaze dropped. Luke tensed. "I gave him this address."

"What?" Frannie shrieked, masking Luke's growl. "Why would you?"

"I didn't know you then, kid. This was way before any of this."

"After that first meeting? In the diner?"

"I followed you long enough to figure out where you were going, then I told Lucian."

Luke's body tensed. That was how he'd beat Luke home from the pub that night. His hands clenched into fists. Ultimately, he knew that Daryl hadn't told the pack master anything he couldn't have figured out by simply tracking his scent. The wolf in him knew that didn't matter though. Daryl had done something that had put his mate in danger. That was unforgivable. He stepped away from Finn and Frannie, not wanting a chance that they could get hurt. He nodded to Sorell before shifting, allowing his body to become fluid, to reform and readjust into his wolf shape. He took two quick steps before leaping toward Daryl. His eyes widened in fear, and he shifted. In his wolf form, he was smaller than Luke and entirely brown, almost more like a shaggy dog than a wolf.

From the corner of his eyes, he saw that Frannie had gotten to her feet. Sorell was at her side, not quite restraining her, but also not allowing her to move any closer. Finn stood as well, but he made no move to stop Luke. His gaze was dark yet trusting. He wasn't used to seeing Luke in this form but trusted him enough to let him do what he thought was needed. Luke didn't need to look for Conner or Pippen. He could sense that they had shifted as well and that they were standing behind him in solidarity.

As he neared, Daryl crouched his head low and looked up at him. He wasn't displaying any acts of dominance, but he wasn't submitting either. Right now, Luke needed total submission.

He growled low in his throat and bared his teeth. Daryl did not immediately react, and Luke punished him by lunging forward biting him just hard enough around the neck so that he would definitely feel it, but wouldn't break the skin. Daryl yelped and dropped, displaying the act of obedience that Luke's wolf needed, that the pack needed if they were going to remain harmonious.

Luke snarled, keeping Daryl in place for a few moments longer before stepping over him and trotting back to where

Finn stood. On all fours, he reached to Finn's chest. He didn't want to scare him, but this was important to him. He hadn't realized how important until he stood as a wolf in front of his mate.

Finn hadn't grown up in the same world, knew next to nothing about being a shifter. Luke needed to educate him, for his safety but also for his approval.

He looked up at him and tried not to be so menacing. He wasn't very good at it. Finn stretched out a trembling hand, palm down, fingers spread. He let his hand hover in the space between them, either unwilling or unable to go the remaining inches that would bring his palm in contact with Luke's muzzle. Luke stretched his neck, erasing the space for him. He wasn't prepared for how amazing his mate's hand would feel in his fur. It wasn't sexual, but more like the world felt even, balanced and harmonious. It was the most natural feeling in the world to have his mate slide his fingers through his fur, down his neck, and down his spine.

Then he patted him twice on the bottom.

"Good boy," Finn said with a devilish wink.

Pippen and Conner both barked. The closest sound to a laugh that a wolf had. Luke let their laughter slide and jumped up on his hind legs, easily landing his front legs on Finn's shoulders. He gave Finn his best wolfy grin and then licked him once, from chin to forehead. Finn's squeal was enough of a reward.

"Yuck, you have dog breath!" he howled. He stepped out from under him and then made the mistake of running.

CHAPTER SIXTEEN

Finn rolled over, casting an arm around Luke's broad chest. Luke held him in a warm embrace as Finn snuggled in. "What time is it?" he mumbled into Luke's armpit.

"Ten thirty," Luke replied. "I've already been up, had breakfast, went with the guys for a run and helped Frannie install that new sound system."

Finn yawned, tired from just hearing everything Luke had achieved so far. "And then you came back?"

"Of course, my mate was still naked and sleeping, how do I pass that chance up?"

"I was naked and sleeping when you got up the first time."

"True, but when I returned there was a better chance of you waking and me being able to do this." Luke held Finn's chin up and kissed him slowly, thoroughly.

Finn felt the kiss from his lips down to his toes. It energized him enough to sit up and consider getting out of bed. But getting out of bed meant, not kissing Luke and that idea made him very tired. He grabbed Luke's biceps, halting him.

"Or, we could stay in, maybe order breakfast, watch a movie?"

Luke smiled, and Finn knew he had him. At that moment there was a rude and urgent knock at his door. "Finners!" Frannie shouted. "Get some pants on and gird those loins. *Mom is coming.*"

Finn yanked from Luke's embrace and stood abruptly. He pulled on a pair of boxers and stomped to the door, ripping it open. "What did you say?"

Frannie stood on the other side, her curly hair a wild mess on her head, a smudge on her cheek most likely from ink. She narrowed her sharp eyes at him. "Are you feeling alright?"

"Of course not!" Finn choked. "Mom is coming?"

Frannie pushed his door open and barged all the way into his room. "Yes, she is, but..."

"What?"

"You've been sleeping in really often lately?" she said the statement like a question.

"Are you mad I didn't do the dishes? I will, okay? Doesn't holding the role of alpha's mate grant me any sort of reprieve?"

"It grants you every reprieve," Luke said from the bed just as Frannie said, "No."

"I'd wash more often if your counters weren't at such weird heights," Finn said, pulling on clothes. "My back hurts all the time these days trying to scrub all the pots and pans. Does Pippen need to use so many dishes?"

"He is practicing," Frannie said offhandedly. She went to his curtains and spread them open letting in a wave of blinding light.

"What did I do to you?" he asked. "That sun is killing my head."

"A headache?" Frannie asked quietly.

"Yeah," he said with an antagonistic sibling tone. "Do you actually have any painkillers on you or are you just going to gawk?"

Frannie stepped backward. "I'm just going to...go look for some." She turned and nearly ran out of the room.

Finn turned to Luke, his hands flung out at his sides in a can-you-believe-that motion. "What is wrong with her?" he asked Luke. "Do you think she is starting to resent us? Me?" He knew he was shrieking, but Frannie had really messed with his head. She was probably just mad that he hadn't been helping out more around the house. It wasn't like he had the excuse of Daryl or even Luke who had both secured legal employment at the garage in the community.

Luke had basically put his foot down when it came to Finn finding a job and so he'd been little more than a housewife for the last couple of weeks. Apparently, according to Frannie, he'd been a lazy housewife.

He didn't have much time to worry about all that. Finn saw his mom during their lunches, a few here and there so she wouldn't worry, but she didn't know anything about Finn's love life.

"Those aren't warm and fuzzy feelings I am sensing from you."

"I've never, I mean, my mom doesn't...I've never officially come out to my family."

"Frannie knows."

Finn thought about that. He'd never had the talk with Frannie either, it was simply one of those things she just accepted. She was good with rolling with the punches. Finn would rather run from the punches, very quickly and then hide. He didn't have to tell her today, did he? Maybe he could just say Luke was another roommate. As long as they didn't sit too close—

"I will not hide our relationship like it is something to be ashamed of," Luke said darkly. "I will leave the house if you need me to."

Finn hurried to be by his side. He'd allowed his own weakness to take control. "No, Luke, I'm sorry. I don't want you to leave, I don't want us to hide. She'll just have to accept it too, or she can not accept it. I don't care." He grabbed Luke's hand, squeezing his fingers, sliding his touch upward to his forearm, further to his biceps. "My mood is all over the place lately, please forgive me."

"Of course," came his rumbled reply.

In minutes Finn was dressed and standing next to Luke in the living room. Why did it feel so awkward? Did they wait by the front door to greet her? What, like she's a visiting dignitary or something? But then, it would be rude to just sit in the living room watching television. He'd gone so long without experiencing this freezing social anxiety. It made him feel less equipped to handle it.

"Whoa, boss," Sorell said, appearing from the hallway. "You okay? Need a coffee?"

"My mother is—"

His mom's little four-door pulled into the driveway. Finn grabbed hold of Luke's hand tightly, watching her park. His mouth dropped. His oldest brother, Felix, stepped out of the passenger side. Finn watched his mom hurry to Felix's side. Why was he here? Last Finn had heard, Felix had been off being an amazing doctor for very poor children in some horribly deprived country. Finn stumbled back with the shock of seeing Felix. The two of them hadn't been in the same room for at least a year, and he absolutely hadn't seen Finn since his time in the institution.

Growing up, Finn had been happiest melting into the background. That became easier with the arrival of the little ham, Frannie. But for some reason, Felix was always pushing him, always putting Finn in situations that made him uncomfortable and for that reason, Finn avoided him as much as he could. Finn found Frannie hurrying toward them. She'd changed into a summer dress and had braided her wild hair back.

"Holy shit, Felix?" Frannie said as she looked through the window. "I swear I didn't know, Finn."

"Why, who is he?" Luke asked, instantly growing tense and alert.

They were at the door now, there was a short series of knocks. Frannie swung her door open, and Felix burst inside, lifting her up easily into a bear hug and swinging her once in a circle.

"Oof!" Frannie squealed. "Put me down before you drop me!" Their mother stepped in with a huge smile on her face. "So this is why you had to come over, and it had to be today," Frannie said to their mom, giving her a hug.

Finn's mom found him immediately. Finn tried not to cringe as he watched her face. She had worry in her eyes, like always, but then her gaze went to where Finn held Luke's hand, and her eyes narrowed. Too slowly, she met his eyes again, and sure enough, there was a tightness in them.

Finn was happy he hadn't shrunk back from her evaluation, had kept a steady hold of his alpha's hand. But now, he stepped away from him and hugged his mother. "It is really good to see you, Mom," he said, surprised by how much he meant it.

"You too, sweetie." She pulled back and stared at him from arm's length. "You look...different. Happier." She smiled.

"This is Luke," Finn said, going back to Luke's side. "He is my ma—boyfriend." Finn exchanged a quick, silent plea, with Luke.

"Finners!" Felix said loudly, stepping up between them. "It is so great to see you again." He gave him a quick bro hug and then turned to Luke and extended his hand. "Hey there, I'm the big brother, Felix."

"When did you get back?" Finn asked, pleased with how well everything was going so far.

"Last night. Our team got pulled out, civil unrest. I was up for some time off, so I thought, why not reconnect with the family before getting reassigned?"

Just then, Pippen entered with Conner at his heels. Pippen had put on one of Frannie's frilly purple aprons and held a casserole dish. "Brunch is served," he said proudly. Sorell sauntered forward as Daryl came in through the open front door, rubbing his greasy hands on the front of his jeans.

"Francesca," their mother said, tightly. "Who are all these people?"

IT TOOK Finn's mother one bite of Pippen's spinach and swiss quiche to decide it was alright with her if Frannie had a few extra roommates. Of course, Frannie had spun it in such a way that it seemed like they were all paying to live here. Like she was benefiting from the extra money. Now, they sat around the kitchen table, eating the quiche, sausage, and croissants.

"You know, Ma, it is good you are here," Frannie said, out of nowhere. "I've been getting these horrible headaches lately. Don't you suffer from migraines?"

Their mother nodded. Finn took another bite, worried for his sister. He didn't know she'd been getting headaches too.

"And my back, especially my lower back has been really acting up. Even though I haven't done much of anything around the house since I've been so sleepy lately."

Their mother stared at Frannie, concern on her features. Then, she smiled really wide, wider than Finn had ever seen. "Oh Frannie, you have a boyfriend now? You're pregnant?"

"What? No. But why do you ask?"

"Oh, sorry, just that you should probably get tested, sounds like you might be pregnant, honey."

Frannie put her fork down and looked at Finn head-on, unblinking. "Oh really? Pregnant you say?" she said without breaking eye contact.

Finn's fork clattered to the table. The quiche rolled in his stomach and started a turbo train journey back up his esophagus. "I think I'm going to be sick," he said before running to the bathroom.

LUKE HEARD Finn pacing on the other side of the bathroom door. A better noise than the retching and puking he'd witnessed a minute or so ago. He'd been only half paying attention to Frannie as he'd been so keyed on making sure Finn was okay with the sudden appearance of his older brother but he'd gotten the gist of what she'd been asking. He was also very good at putting two and two together.

Luke wasn't sure if he was going to shout and start buying cigars or if he was going to need to nudge Finn over for a space in front of the toilet. He knocked gently on the door. "Finn? Babe?"

"What?" The question was quiet and a little wary.

"Can I come in?"

"I don't know, can you?"

Luke grinned. Finn was scared, that was obvious, but he still had an attitude, which was a good sign. He opened the door and stepped in, silently shutting the door again behind him. Finn sat on the edge of the bathtub, his forehead braced against his hands. Luke moved to the space in front of him, dropping to his knees so he could look into his mate's face. "Hey," he tugged at a hand. "Look at me."

"I know we sort of discussed this all before, but it seemed very, just talk, back then. Like something that could maybe happen. I have so many questions. So many worries. And I feel like crying, but I also sort of want to punch you. But then at the same time, I want to take a nap."

Luke bit the insides of his cheeks to keep from smiling. He felt like he might explode from his elation.

"When you look at me like that, it makes me want to punch you more than nap."

"Like what, babe?"

"Like the cat who caught the canary. Or the cat that had sex with the canary and then got the canary pregnant."

"That is a gross and offensive analogy. I am not a cat person." He couldn't help the wide smile he knew was plastered across his face. He probably looked like a grinning idiot but didn't care. He pulled Finn against him, feeling his body line up perfectly with his. Meeting this amazing man had been the best day of his life that just kept proving itself better and better. "I should go," he said abruptly. "To the store."

"For cigarettes?" Finn asked wryly.

Luke growled quietly at the implication. "No, mate. For a test."

"Oh, good idea. Could you do me a favor first and ask Frannie to come in? After she says bye to Mom and Felix."

"You're staying in the bathroom?" Luke asked.

Finn nodded, there was a little pink to his cheeks. "I'm still feeling a little nauseous."

Luke left the bathroom, wanting to quickly find Frannie so he could get the test and maybe some ginger ale. He nearly ran into Felix, skulking down the hallway.

"Oh, hey sorry. I was just looking for Finn to say bye."

"He's not feeling well, sorry."

Felix looked down at the carpet. He was either sad to not be able to say goodbye, or he was lying. Luke stepped toward him, getting into his space. He was a pretty big guy and generally, just imposing on another person's space was enough to get them to rethink or confess. Felix didn't back down though. He caught Luke's gaze.

"I am really glad to have met you. I've never seen Finn look happier. He was always so...uncomfortable. He could never sit in one place, stayed to the walls, afraid someone would notice him. He's a great kid. A great guy, and with you...I don't know. It's like he is glowing." If he was lying, he was a master at it. He sounded genuine. He looked past Luke to someone who'd come up behind them in the hallway. "I, uh, I gotta go now. With mom. Nice to meet you." He turned and hurried away. Luke looked behind him to see who'd had him running away like a kicked dog.

Sorell sauntered toward him, his hands shoved in his pockets. "What's up, boss?"

Luke smiled. "Want to go with me to the store?"

LUKE RETURNED thirty minutes later with his arms full of bags, Sorell's as well. He plopped it all down on the couch opposite where Finn was sitting. He'd made it out of the bathroom at least.

"How many tests did you buy?" he asked looking at the bags with wonder.

"Well, I bought a few of those cause I thought what if one was defective? And then I got you some ginger ale, and Sorell said that when his pack mate was pregnant, she couldn't get enough salted caramel cookies. And then a heating pad for your back and I was going to get some painkillers for your headache, but the lady said to be careful with that and to try lavender oil first. And a soft blanket, peppermint tea, slippers and—" he stopped listing his items, mostly because Frannie and Finn were laughing too loudly to hear him anyway.

Frannie grabbed the test from him. "We'll see you in 3-5 minutes."

He idly wondered how Frannie knew how long a pregnancy test took but then figured that was just the type of information girls grew up knowing. He and Finn would be doing this on a learning curve. But they had Frannie. And they would find a shifter doctor. Luke stopped thinking when Finn reappeared with Frannie behind him. He saw Frannie's smile first, then saw Finn's face. He looked, there were no words. Amazing? Perfect? They didn't quite cover the soft smile that played on his lips, the color that kissed his cheeks, the fire and light in his eyes. His Finn, his mate.

"Are you?" Luke couldn't finish, his throat closed up with emotion.

He nodded. Luke roared and flew to him, lifting him up and spinning him in a circle. Finn threw his head back and laughed, and then Frannie smacked Luke in the arm saying he needed to be careful. Luke set Finn down oh-so-gently, keeping his arms braced around him like a protective cage. The rest of their pack arrived then, Sorell at the head.

Pippen clasped his hands in front of his body. "So? Are we having a celebratory dinner or a normal dinner?"

"Celebratory," Luke said.

The pack cheered, even Daryl, and rushed forward to congratulate them. After everyone had hugged everyone else, they sat in the living room. Luke held Finn half on his lap, Frannie was next to him with her feet propped up on Conner as he sat on the floor in front of her. On the other couch, Pippen, Sorell, and Daryl squished together. Luke let himself look at the group of people, looked at their smiles. He hadn't realized how lonely he had been until he wasn't anymore. He knew now that finding Finn had been the most important thing he'd ever do.

CHAPTER SEVENTEEN

FINN PROPPED his legs up on a pillow Luke had gotten them expressly for that purpose.

"Okay," Frannie said, balancing a package of cookies on top of a carton of double mint chocolate chip. "I've got the snacks, we've put in the movie, and the guys are all out for at least two hours." She settled in on the opposite end of the couch, handing Finn the ice cream and a spoon while reaching down to scoop up her own glass of wine. She'd rented the latest horror flick, Werewolves vs. Zombies, much to the annoyance of just about every other occupant of the house.

Finn took a creamy spoonful and let it settle on his tongue. His body had settled, no more crazy urgings and his senses had dulled, though Luke had guessed that would just be the case during the pregnancy. *The pregnancy.* That was still a hard one to get his head around. The aches and pains and nausea he could do without, but being able to indulge his every food craving? That was a pretty awesome perk to being pregnant with his alpha mate's baby or babies. The first ultrasound hadn't been very clear, but everyone agreed it wasn't unusual for shifter women to have more than one baby at a time, usually two, occasionally three. They were scheduled back tomorrow. There were still a lot of unanswered questions, but Finn had faith that the shifter doctor Luke had contacted, Dr. Roods, would be able to answer most of their questions and that the rest would sort itself out. It wasn't that he had faith in the world to look out for him, but he had faith in Luke to always do what was best and safest for him. It was a weird and amazing feeling.

The opening credits just began to roll when there was a sharp knock at the door. Frannie paused the screen, her hand slipping under the sofa cushion. Normally, she didn't have reason to still be packing, there was usually someone around, but the rare times when it was her and Finn, she slipped the stupid gun into the nearest hiding space next to her. He'd really have to talk to her about that gun. If they were going to have children in this house, she would need a gun safe. For the moment though, she slipped it in the back of her pants and went to the door, peeking through the hole.

"There's no one there," she mumbled.

"Dong and ditch?"

"Sure, if you were a kid fifty years ago. No one dong and ditches anymore, not innocently." She kept the chain on and opened the door a sliver. She must have been convinced there was no one there because she opened the door and bent down, returning to Finn a moment later holding a brown paper package. "It's addressed to you. No return address though."

"That's weird."

"Don't open it, Finners. Wait for Luke."

"Your wild mind, great when you're writing a book but—"

"Do not discount me. At least examine the thing. Oil marks? Residue? Powder?"

Finn looked the package over. There was nothing out of the ordinary. It looked for all the world to be a normal brown cardboard box. He used the other end of his spoon to slice the packing tape and unfolded the cardboard panels. There was a small white envelope nestled on the top of what looked like an industrial strength plastic freezer bag. He couldn't see inside. The plastic was so thick and murky. He opened the card, his eyes widening after the first line. He felt weak and light headed.

"What? Finn? What? You've gone all pale."

Finn's voice shook as he read over the messy scrawl. "Dear Finn, I regret our relationship hasn't begun the way I wanted it to. I'd sent what I thought was a trusted man to deliver you to me easily and painlessly. This is the second time I have been let down. And really, it is the second time you have been let down as well as it has kept you from me. I understand you are confused now, please accept this as a gift, from me to you. They were beautiful, but they did not serve their purpose. Besides, I believe that together, we will create a more beautiful pair. Perhaps even a whole litter. With love, Lucian."

"Do not open that bag, Finn. I am ordering you, do not open that—"

Finn ripped the top of the bag open, feeling like the stereotypical girl from a horror movie who went upstairs toward danger instead of downstairs toward the exit. He jerked to his feet, letting the box and its contents fall off his lap and onto the ground. A pair of grotesque, disembodied eyeballs stared cockeyed at him and Frannie, both of them a stunning shade of frozen forest. He almost expected them to blink.

"Oh my god. There are eyeballs on my carpet. Whose eyeballs are on my carpet? Oh my god."

"Frannie! Calm down!" Finn hollered, though his own heartbeat was racing.

Frannie looked at him and blinked, seemingly coming to her senses. "Finn, breathe, slowly. You should sit. You can't get excited—you don't know what it will do to the baby-babies." She helped Finn down on the seat furthest from the eyeballs on the carpet. She squeezed into the space next to them so that they were both cuddled on the love seat. Technically, there wasn't enough room for them both, but Finn did not object, and neither did Frannie.

He put an arm around her shoulders, and she slid one behind his back. Together they stared at the special delivery. Finn felt stunned and figured Frannie did as well. He was just getting used to this world of shifters. He was not used to getting psychotic love letters and body part gifts.

"I know those eyes," he said to Frannie, detached. "The guy from the store who tried to take me. He has...had those eyes."

Frannie cocked her head to the side. "They are striking. Or would be, if they were in someone's head." She sighed. "I guess that is a relief. They aren't from someone else we know."

"I don't feel relieved."

A moment of silence passed between them.

"Me neither," Frannie said finally. "You have to call Luke."

"I don't even know if I want to tell Luke," Finn admitted.

"What?" Frannie shrieked, turning toward him. "Why the hell not?"

Finn couldn't take his eyes off of the eyes. "Because, Frannie, this pack master guy is crazy. This guy worked for him, and now he is a pair of eyeballs on the carpet. What do you think he will do to someone like Luke? Someone he actually doesn't like, who is standing in his way?"

"Luke is a grown man. He can take care of himself."

"And I'm a grown man too. I can take care of him."

"Take care of who?" Pippen asked as he entered. They didn't have a chance to answer him as he saw the eyes on the floor and immediately hardened. He whipped out a switch-blade from his pants. "Conner," he called out urgently.

Conner rushed in from outside, searching for danger, staying near Pippen. He saw the eyes and then the box, and then he straightened. "Are you both okay?" he asked smoothly.

"Yes," Frannie said. "Though, Finn might've gotten hurt in the head somehow since he is talking about not letting Luke know the crazy pack master sent him eyeballs in the mail."

"You don't have to tell him," Conner said, surprising Finn. "But I do." He smiled, saw Finn's scowl and smiled wider. "He is our alpha, Finn. Yours too. It is his job to help protect all of us."

"Who is going to protect him from himself though? He's gonna go ballistic and will want to rush out there to chal-lenge the other alpha."

Pippen stepped around the package. "Don't you realize that will happen eventually, Finn? We'll either move, or he'll have to challenge. What we are doing now, living in the same territory, it is precarious at best."

Finn hadn't thought about it. His hand went to his belly, it wasn't huge, but Finn had always had pretty flat abs, so the little lump there felt substantial. It also reminded him of how fragile and weak he was because of it. He couldn't let it make him helpless though. Finn decided then that he would tell Luke. Really he didn't have a choice. And Luke would do what it took to keep him and the pack safe. Finn promised to himself he'd make sure Luke was safe, no matter what it took.

LUKE CHECKED the front door lock again. He continued on his routine, making sure the kitchen window was latched, moved to the sliding door, ensuring the door was locked and that the bar was placed securely in the sliding grate.

"Luke?" Finn's sleepy voice sounded from behind him. "What are you doing? It's so late."

"Just checking the locks, love. I'll be back to bed soon."

Finn yawned and rubbed his growing belly, looking so fucking adorable Luke's heart squeezed. "You did that already, twice."

"I know, but—"

Finn tugged at his shirt, pulling him gently from the door, from his routine, from his new obsession. "Please come lie with me. That bed feels so big without you these days."

"Well you do sleep in it more often," he teased.

"And your job at the shop keeps you away during the day," Finn said with a fake pout.

"We're fortunate Daryl could get me in at the garage," he said but then leaned in to give Finn a peck on the cheek. He was lucky that sleepy Finn had shown up and not angry Finn. For some reason, seeing Luke do certain things like checking the locks or inspect the car before getting into it made Finn upset sometimes.

Luke figured he just didn't like feeling like he was too babied. But, when you had a baby inside of you, it was okay to be babied. Luke settled a flat palm over Finn's stomach.

They had gone to see the shifter doctor that day for their second ultrasound and he'd told them everything looked fine, that their little baby was growing healthy. Dr. Rood had even said he'd seen cases of males giving birth before. It was not as common as Luke had thought initially, but it wasn't unheard of. A shifter pregnancy took about four months, and when the time came, Finn would have a c-section and Luke would finally meet the little miracle.

Finn was finally going to let him take him to the baby store where they were going to pick up everything they needed for little...*Demetrius?* He'd offer the name as an idea.

His biggest, most beloved job now though, was keeping his mate happy. He guided him down on the bed, quickly following behind and pulling him against his body. Finn rolled over so that they faced each other. He had a playful look in his eyes that Luke recognized. His cock recognized it too, instantly springing to attention.

"I feel like it's been forever," Finn mumbled, reaching for the elastic band of Luke's pants. "I miss it. I miss you wanting me."

"I never stopped wanting you," Luke said, a little surprised. He'd been preoccupied with the pregnancy and making sure the house was safe and secure, but he'd never stopped desiring Finn. He saw there was want in his expression now. His lips parted, his pupils had dilated. "I wanted you before, I'll want you after. Even when we are both so sleep deprived we don't know our own names."

"But I want you now," Finn whispered, drawing the last word out until it sounded like a plea.

His mate didn't need to beg for sex, but it didn't feel bad against his ears. Luke let his hands wander over Finn's body, sliding up his thighs, bypassing his most sensitive part and letting his fingers brush over his stomach. Pride welled up inside him along with his lust. His love, his world. Luke nibbled at the back of Finn's neck, tweaking his nipples. His mate gave a breathy moan. He laid his palm against Finn's chin, bringing his lips around. Luke kissed him, slowly, exploring. He let his tongue reacquaint itself with every corner of his mouth, his lower teeth, licking along the top of his mouth. He tasted like mint likely left over from his toothpaste. Finn sucked on his tongue, a carnal reproduction of what Luke's cock would soon be doing.

"Oh, my love, have I been neglecting you? I'll have to make up for that. Tonight, I'll make you sore."

FINN WHIMPERED. They'd both gotten so caught up with the pregnancy, the pack and keeping the house safe that it had been longer than ever since the last time he'd felt his love deep inside him. Luke's fingers danced over his cock now, an erotic fingertip ballet from tip to base. Somehow, his cock hardened, straining up and searching. Finn bit his lip. They had a full house these days. A full house of people with heightened senses.

"What are you doing?" Luke asked, propping himself up on one elbow.

"I don't want to make too much noise," he whispered back.

Luke responded with a firm grip on Finn's cock, letting it slide slowly down, squeezing the whole way. Finn shuddered and moaned. "How many times do I need to tell you not to censor yourself? Not with me. Never with me." He pumped him again, letting some of the liquid that had spurted out lubricate his path.

"But it's just polite—"

Luke quickened the pace of his hand job, cutting off Finn's words. "Your sister sleeps with headphones and everyone else is used to distracting themselves. They aren't new to sensitive hearing."

That made sense. Shifters, unless they were lone, usually lived in close quarters. But that didn't mean he wouldn't get payback for Luke silencing his words with sex. Payback could wait though, because Luke was readjusting his body, sliding himself into position. Finn felt the tip of Luke's cock nudge against his hole. Next, he felt that amazing burst of liquid as it dripped down, lubricating and sensitizing his back entrance.

"I'm going to have to start you off slow," Luke murmured, pulling away.

Finn lamented the loss of heat and strained back to get it back. Luke made a tsking noise. His finger replaced the spot where his cock had been. He rubbed and massaged Finn, relaxing and preparing him for his large member. He slid the finger in slowly, Finn felt each digit impale him and agreed. It had been a long time. But soon, his ass was greedy again, wanting more than just the one finger. Luke accommodated him, adding another finger and letting them both slide in inch by inch. Inside, he wiggled, massaging his g-spot. Finn yelped and bit his pillow.

"My mate, this was unforgivable of me." He repositioned so that they both lay on their sides, Luke spooning Finn. He let the huge head of his cock press in. It pushed past his outer ring, so much bigger and more demanding than his fingers had been. Finn would've felt stretched too tight if his alpha's lubricating cum hadn't continued to do its magic, helping to soften the pain he might have felt and letting him concentrate on the pleasure.

And there was so much pleasure to concentrate on. Blinding, white-hot, being filled by Luke was like being in the middle of an erotic supernova. Finn felt his body do the one thing it had been made for, to accept its mate. Soon, Luke urged himself in all the way, his balls brushed the bottom of Finn's ass, his stomach rested against his back. He stayed that way, an arm reaching around Finn's body to anchor him there. The other hand held him at his hip to ensure that he would remain still. He breathed heavy and hard into Finn's ear.

"This is where I will always belong. Right here, inside of you."

"Yes," Finn said, but it turned into a wail as Luke pulled out only to thrust back inside.

He set a dizzying pace, slamming into Finn with a passion that was animalistic. The bed creaked and groaned below them. Finn grunted, high pitched and needy as he accepted the intrusion over and over. Luke had not been lying, he would be sore the next day, and he would love every moment of it because it would remind him of this time right now when his love was using him in the most loving way possible. Using him while also giving so much. Without even stroking himself Finn felt his orgasm build and quickly break. His release shot out landing on his stomach and the sheet. He bit into the pillow, loving how primal it made him feel.

His alpha pumped once more, but feeling his mate come must have been too much for him. He rammed inside, his hands went to Finn's hips as he held his body tight, letting his cum coat Finn's tight channel.

Without moving, Luke pulled the blanket so that it covered both of their bodies. He let go of Finn's hips and wrapped his arms around him.

"We should change..."

"Shh," Luke said, his lips pressed against Finn's neck. "Tomorrow we will. Just let me sleep now, inside you."

Finn couldn't say no to something like that. He nestled back, loving the warmth and strength of his alpha's chest. Luke was giving him tiny angel's kisses over the back of his neck and shoulders. Soon, his eyelids felt heavy, and Finn fell asleep.

FINN WAS BEING SMOTHERED by a sea of pinks and blues. A visual assault that had him leaning back on his heels. Luke bumped into him, not expecting his abrupt stop.

"What?" he asked, spinning around in a protective move that had Finn behind him and shielded.

Finn stepped to the side. "Nothing so serious. Just..." He waved at the rows and rows in front of him. He never knew so much baby stuff existed. "*Damn.*"

Luke settled and pulled out his list. He grabbed a cart. "We can start at the top?" he suggested doubtfully.

"Diapers," Finn said without any follow-up. He shrugged. "I think diapers are the most important thing."

"Shifter mothers when I was a child often used cloth diapers."

Finn stared at him. He had nothing against cloth diapers, he just didn't have anything for them either. "Maybe the formula is more important than diapers. Got to have something to poop."

Luke laughed. "I like your reasoning."

They found the formula aisle, fought about what brand and then finally put a case of one in the cart.

Luke grabbed a few stray cans in other brands. "Just in case little Demetrius doesn't like the flavor of that one."

Finn stopped in his tracks. "Little who?"

Luke smiled. "I like it. I think it is stately."

"And if it is a girl?"

"Demetria?"

Finn shook his head. "No. No way. I am not setting my kid up for failure. Besides, why don't we go with a nice F name like my mother?"

"Felix, Farley, Finn, Francesca," Luke ticked off the names of Finn and his siblings, raising a finger with each one. "And Filbert?"

"Ugh, no. Point taken." Finn followed Luke into the bottle aisle. "I had a grandpa when I was very young that I remember. He was very nice to me. Not like my horrid grandma who used to make me dress up and perform songs for her friends. She stopped after the first time I puked all over her carpet."

Luke laughed and grabbed a pack of bottles with a label that professed the nipple was "like the real thing."

Finn snorted.

"What was his name?" Luke asked.

"Phillip."

Luke considered the name. "I don't hate it. I could see myself yelling it as I cheer him on during football."

"Phillip won't like sports," Finn said, offended.

Luke plopped an arm over his shoulders. "Of course he will. And he will like reading. He will be the perfect mixture of us."

Finn thought he might cry from happiness. He cleared his throat. "And if it is a girl?"

"Serena Ann, like my mother," Luke said quietly, and Finn knew the name was perfect.

CHAPTER EIGHTEEN

FINN PUSHED OPEN the door to Dr. Rood's office. Frannie followed him, supposedly there to help but she had her head down, her mind somewhere else entirely. Luke was going to come soon but had to finish up at the garage first. He and Daryll were in high demand down there. But, he'd said he would be here so Finn knew he would be.

Finn felt his small hairs rise on his arms and at the back of his neck. He surveyed the empty room. Dr. Roods serviced shifters and humans, and his waiting room was usually full of both types.

Now, every chair was empty, even the desk was vacant. He stepped into the eerie space. "Frannie?"

"Hm?" She looked up from her phone, noticed his expression and then looked around the room, quickly putting two and two together. "Stay close," she said, moving in front of him.

Finn rolled his eyes. Luke's protective streak was wearing off on the whole house. Being with child didn't help, but truthfully, it wasn't extremely noticeable. If he wore an over-sized zip-up sweater like he was today, then anyone passing him wouldn't even notice.

Still, she was in front of him when they moved together back to the patient room. He'd been in the room a handful of times in the last two and a half months and was half sure that Dr. Roods would be sitting in there waiting for him with his wise and patient smile. Finn ran into Frannie's back. She hissed and turned around, pushing him.

"Go, Finn, go!" She urged him away, but Finn was taller and looked over her head into the room. At first, he didn't recognize what he was looking at. It resembled an odd portrait or artistic piece, a weird bouquet of flowers. But they weren't flowers, they were spatters of blood. His eyes followed the grotesque garden down to the lifeless form of Dr. Roods.

He fell back. Overwhelming terror made him unsteady. As did Frannie's pushing. He caught his footing and turned, charging forward to run. He slammed right into a solid body and yelped, falling away. Luke caught him before he could hit the ground and cradled his shaking form to his front. "Finn, Finn, are you hurt?" he searched over every part of Finn that he could see. "I can smell..." He looked to Frannie who indicated with a shaky nod the direction of where the smell was coming from. He looked torn, unsure as to if he should keep Finn clutched to his front or put him down. He ended up setting Finn down by the wall on the outside of the door. He disappeared inside the room of horrors. The room was silent, and soon Luke came back out holding a white envelope. Finn's name was written on the front with a large ridiculous heart drawn around it. He gasped, not believing till that moment that he hadn't put two and two together more quickly.

Lucian. He'd found out about Finn's doctor, he'd found

him and killed him. But Finn was so close to his due date. How would they find another shifter-friendly doctor so quickly? He felt like he couldn't breathe, gasping for air in a room that smelled too much like blood. He knew what blood smelled like. He felt transported back to that life-changing moment, his wrist, bathed in tangy blood that seeped from his own body. His vision blurred and warped, going in and out of focus as it moved from side to side. He was going to be sick.

"I'm here, Finn," he heard his mate mumble in his ear. At that moment, Luke's voice was the only one that he would have been able to pay attention to. His touch acted like a balm, numbing his frazzled senses and cooling his nerves. Luke carried him, herding Frannie in front of them, out of the office building. He was on his phone, talking in low tones.

Minutes later, Sorell and Pippen walked across the parking lot. "I want you two to take Frannie and Finn back to the house. Pippen, you are on guard. Sorell, you drive."

"Wait, where are you going? Where will you be?" Finn's question sounded whiny.

"Love, I can't let this go any longer. People are getting hurt. He is escalating."

"This is what he wants!"

"It's what we both want," he said with finality.

Finn remembered the conversation he'd had with Pippen, about two alphas living so close together. Luke had been aching for this fight? Was he just using Finn as an excuse? He immediately discounted that thought. Luke did whatever it took to keep Finn safe. If he hadn't met Finn originally, he probably would've shipped out of town. But he had stayed in town, and every day, his inner animal urged him to conquer that other wolf. And now he would try, but what if it was a trap?

"You can't go, Luke, please."

Luke led him to the back of the car, away from the others. Frannie was telling Sorell what they'd seen while Pippen had his elf eyes scanning every inch of the parking lot.

"Mate, it is in my nature to keep you safe. To keep our family safe. You can't ask me not to do that." He spoke low and stared into Finn's eyes with a pleading expression. He needed Finn to realize that this was an innate part of him. To deny him this urge was like denying part of him.

"I'm scared."

"Such little faith?" Luke puffed up a little, broadening his chest. Finn thought he might even have been flexing.

"No, you are strong, like semi-truck strong. But you aren't superman. You can't stop a bullet."

"Shifters don't use guns."

"This shifter is crazy."

"We're all kind of crazy."

Finn would not smile. Only his mate could make him almost smile at a time like this. "It could be a trap."

Luke cupped his face. Kissed him gently, tenderly and then let his hands fall to Finn's stomach, caressing him lovingly. "I'm sure it is a trap. That doesn't change this. Dr. Roods didn't deserve this. Next time it will be someone closer. Sorell? Frannie?"

Finn felt the breath rush out of him at the thought of Frannie getting hurt, of her blood decorating walls. He couldn't respond. He didn't have the air or the words. Luke was right.

Luke kissed him, chastely on the forehead, settled him in the back of Frannie's car and shut the door. He murmured something to Sorell, and then with a final wave, got in his own car. Finn closed his eyes, pushing the tears back. Luke was strong, smart. He'd come back to him. He had to come back to him.

The four of them were silent the entire way back to Frannie's house. They'd passed a handful of cop cars, sirens blaring, speeding in the opposite direction. Luke must have called in a tip or maybe, another patient had shown up. Finn didn't like the idea of some unsuspecting person also being scarred because of him. Even if it was just emotionally.

Finn stepped out of the car and then doubled over, his hands supporting his stomach. Pippen was by his side. His bright eyes looked him over.

"What is it, boss?" he asked in his high, soft voice.

Finn shook his head. "Nothing, just a twinge. Let's get inside, I think there is a carton of ice cream with my name on it." Because Finn wasn't sure what else he was supposed to do while he worried over Luke. He'd already realized that he would have to actually work out on a schedule after, if he wanted his naturally fit body back.

Pippen grinned and grabbed his arm to escort him. Then, out of nowhere, he dropped it, fell to a crouch and hissed. "Get in the car," he ordered. Sorell and Frannie were almost to the door when it opened. Lucian walked out of their house, smiling, looking every bit like the handsome villain cast in the latest Hollywood blockbuster. Finn had slid in the front seat. He sat there now and watched Sorell push Frannie behind him protectively as Lucian's pack started stepping out of the perimeter. They were nearly surrounded.

"No one has to get hurt," Lucian said loudly, just like a

villain would say in a moment like that. "Give me Finn, and we'll leave, just like that."

"Never," Frannie seethed, but Finn saw her limbs shaking.

She was terrified, out in the open while Finn was hiding inside the car. Lucian looked at her like he'd just noticed her. "You tried to shoot me," he observed. "Where is that gun now?"

Frannie straightened, and Finn wanted to punch himself. He'd all but demanded she leave the gun at home saying that Luke would join them. "Like I would tell you. Or maybe I will. It's in the car. No. It's in my room," she said and then, "Oh now I remember I left it up your ass."

Finn knew the gun wasn't in the car, but also knew Frannie was trying to tell him something. He opened the hinge slowly.

Lucian lifted his beautiful face up to the sky and laughed. "You are funny. I'm going to be sad when I have to tear your tongue from your body in front of your brother because he won't do the right thing and come with me."

Finn abandoned his plan to go slow. His search took on a frantic pace. He pulled the glove box open. Out popped a stack of napkins, a bottle of hand sanitizer, some random paperwork and then a spare set of keys.

He pulled the seatbelt around his body and then jammed the keys into the ignition, and every single shifter around them heard. They lunged forward even as Finn revved the engine, not before he heard Lucian say his name like he was bored and not about to get run over.

Finn slammed his foot on the gas, swerving away from Frannie and Sorell, he drove the car forward, slamming into the spot Lucian had stood while plummeting a good foot into the entryway. The impact had Finn slamming forward even as he doubled over to try and protect his stomach. Only his head hit the dash, but the pain was blinding, dumbing.

He couldn't tell which way was up, surrounded by dust and debris. Someone cursed, someone else shouted. Finn blinked. He began to be able to see shapes and light. Sorell was pushing him out of the driver's seat to the passenger. Frannie's fast fingers dabbed at his forehead.

"Drive, Sorell," Pippen commanded.

"I broke your house," Finn said dazedly.

"I am going to break the rest of you as soon as we get out of this," Frannie said, her voice full of emotion. "What was that? What kind of fucking plan was that? A shit plan."

"Frannie, don't—" Finn couldn't speak anymore, he felt a sharp tearing at his gut and then a white-hot pain seared up his spine. He screamed and arched back. "Noooo!" he yelled because he knew, instinctively, he knew what that pain was. The baby was in trouble, it needed out. "Frannie, help me!"

He saw her in the rearview mirror, on the phone. She shouted a direction to Sorell who looked white-faced and worried. Another arrow of pain shot through his body, and then he couldn't see anything. He bent over, throwing up all over his lap and the car. This was going to kill him.

Where was Luke? He could save them. Could save him. *Stupid, so stupid.* There had been a trap. Only, it hadn't been for Luke. It was for Finn, and now he would die, taking the one amazing thing he'd done with him. He closed his eyes and concentrated on breathing. If he was breathing, he was alive. He rubbed his scar, proof that he could live even when he was at his own worst. Because he hadn't slipped, not really. He'd known what he was doing, what was going on. But he'd lived through it. He would live through this.

"Finn?" Felix's deep voice was the last voice Finn thought he would hear at that moment. He grabbed him, pulling him on a stretcher. "Frannie, what kind of joke is this? You said an emergency C-section, you said the patient wouldn't be safe in a hospital."

Frannie moved to Finn's side and unzipped his jacket. "And that is all true. Felix, you have questions, ask them after you save our brother."

"Holy shit."

"Very astute, Felix. You sure this place is secure?"

They were rolling then, the air was suddenly cooler. Finn thought they must have gone inside someplace air-conditioned.

"Yes, it is a free clinic with strict hours. No one will be here now. I don't know what I am dealing with here, Fran. I've never...I mean..."

"Treat it the same as all the other C-sections you've done." That was Sorell, anxiety lined every word.

"I've never done one outside of medical school," Felix admitted.

"Holy shit," Sorell replied.

Finn could've laughed if another blinding knife swipe of pain hadn't sliced straight down his body. From head to toe, he felt it, tearing his muscle from the bone. His throat felt raw, and he realized it was because of his screaming.

"Move aside," Felix ordered. His voice had changed, almost to an emotionless level.

Finn felt a sharp bite, a laughable level of pain compared to what he was experiencing and then, miraculously, his head felt like it was on a cloud. "But...I wanted to..." and then Finn could say no more as he was pulled deep under.

Luke was a fool. He pulled up at home, the place he'd tried to make a sanctuary of peace for his mate and found it in tatters. The yard was torn up from many feet and tire treads. The front porch looked like the gaping mouth of a child who needed braces. Jagged and broken, something horrible had happened there, and Luke hadn't been there to prevent it. Daryl and Conner were at his sides, as stunned as he was.

Luke had been on his way to Lucian's home base, he wasn't stupid though and had had Daryl meet him on the way. Conner was with Daryl when he'd called. Now, the three of them were speechless and searching.

"They're not in there," Daryl said, sniffing the air in front of them.

But they had been. Their scents lingered, as did the scents of more than a dozen shifters, including Lucian's. Luke couldn't help it. He shifted, needing his animal more than his animal needed him. He bent his head back and howled. It would scare the neighbors, but he didn't care.

Daryl and Conner shifted as well, animal instinct, and joined him in his howl. Nose in the air, Luke let his wolf take almost complete control as he searched for a scent to track, the scent that would bring him to his mate. He found it and although he wanted to hold his breath from smelling, that scent would bring him to his mate. He let it fill him and then followed the direction it went, running after the sharp, bitter scent of his mate's pain.

They ran a few miles. Staying out of sight had been impossible. There would be news reports for sure. Luke could not care less. The closer he got the clearer his mate's scent became and what Luke sensed drove him crazy. Pain.

Utter and absolute. Nothing like the hungry need he'd felt from him before. This was edged with danger and impending death. He skidded to a stop at a clinic that looked like it was closed. Luke shifted, mid-step, and continued to follow Finn's scent when he was slammed from the side. He grunted, crashing against the pavement.

"I knew you'd be coming soon," Lucian said. He'd let his claws show, and when he spoke, Luke saw his fangs. "I thought at first to just go in and take him, but this is better." He was suspended somewhere between human and wolf, looking so much like those stupid werewolf movie monsters. Luke hated him even more now.

Hate or not, he didn't have time to battle it out, not when his mate was on the other side of that wall, needing him. "Go away, Lucian, we'll do this properly, with the pack in attendance."

"Listen to you and your old pack traditions. I don't give a shit about all of that. You know, if I have one regret in all this it is that you won't have to experience what I did when I lost my sweet angel. Do you know what it is like to be cleaved in two? You should be thanking me, Luke. You won't live long enough to feel that pain." Lucian relaxed abruptly. "Or, maybe he isn't that important to you? You've lived most your life alone. Walk away. How 'bout this, I'll even give you any little pups that come out of him. I don't give a shit."

Luke and his wolf were one. He didn't care that the babbling man in front of him was an alpha or that he was clearly insane from grief. He was threatening his mate, threatening their offspring, making a claim on what was his. It was unacceptable. Luke moved with no indication that he was going to. He punched, strong and true, cutting his own knuckles against Lucian's teeth. Lucian's head snapped back as many of his teeth exploded from his mouth like a sparkler. There was a snapping sound, and when his body whipped back forward, Lucian's head flopped forward, his neck broken and his body limp. Luke didn't take any time to gloat over his kill, it wasn't honorable or how he'd wanted it done. Lucian's pack wouldn't accept it, but none of that mattered to Luke now.

He spun as if Lucian had been a small detour and followed Finn's scent to a small side door. It was locked. Somewhere down the building wall, glass broke. Conner disappeared through the window, and a minute later, the door opened. Luke went through, ignoring everything else as all of the scents bombarded him. His mate, pain, fear, it bit at his tongue and burned the roof of his mouth. Then there was blood and antiseptic.

Luke opened a swinging door and felt his body turn into stone. On the other side of the large window, his Finn lay lifeless on a gurney, the sheet at his stomach stained red. Frannie was turned away from him, hunched over and shuddering like she was sobbing. But, Luke couldn't seem to look away from the pale, still face of his mate. The beautiful color, the glow that had surrounded him, was gone. He looked ashen...dead.

A man, Felix, walked into view then, his front covered in blood. Luke roared and started forward. Daryl held his arms, daring to stop him.

"Listen, son, listen," he said repeatedly.

Luke stalked forward, slowly into the room, no one noticed his entrance and then he did listen. A soft cry, a shush and an even louder cry. Frannie turned around. She'd been hunched over but because she'd been holding Luke's child. He knew it for what it was. His offspring, his baby. It was beautiful, and yet, Luke couldn't enjoy it, not until he knew for sure that his ears weren't deceiving him, that he really was hearing a slow, steady heart that beat out his soul's song. Even as he stepped forward, that song was growing quieter, slowing.

"Finn," he whispered, going to his love's side. "Finn, please, you have to be alright. I need you. All of this, it's meaningless without you by me. The pack, all of it. I'm a lone wolf without you. I'm alone without you."

CHAPTER NINETEEN

Finn was floating. Above himself? Inside himself? He couldn't reach out and get a steady grip on location, time, or place. He felt disconnected, incorporeal, and free. In the distance, he heard a baby's cry, and his soul lunged toward it, but it was so far away, and he was so very weightless. He wanted to get back down to where he belonged. The sky had opened up and blinded him with its light.

Then he felt it. Felt him. A strong hand, the only thing in the world that he could feel, squeezed his fingers and showed him that he could move, he could control where he went. He used its strength and went back down, following that gently luring voice, knowing that he would follow that voice wherever it went.

Finn's eyes fluttered behind his eyelids. He tried opening them and found them still a little too heavy.

"He's coming out of it," a clinical, yet familiar voice said.

"That's right, baby, slow, take your time, but listen to me, always listen to me."

So bossy.

There was a chuckle, and Finn wondered if he had

spoken out loud. He tried to turn his head toward the sweet sound but found he still didn't have that much control. He whimpered, intensely disliking being so helpless.

"You're safe, mate. I'm here. Take my strength, use my strength."

He had been, and the truth was, Luke was more than strong enough for the two of them. He concentrated on his hand, still holding his prisoner, the light kisses he felt crossed his cheek over his nose to the other cheek. His eyelids fluttered, artificial light, not the blinding pure white light of before, shone through. Then, another sound, the sweet cry of a newborn. His eyes flew open. He found his mate, right beside him. His kind face was full of worry and then in his arms he saw a small bundle of blanket. It was so much more than that. Luke's smile dazzled. He leaned forward so that Finn could see and then he placed the little bundle on his chest.

The tiniest little cheek pressed against his skin. The baby stopped crying instantly and sighed, warm and content. "It's a...it's a..." Finn couldn't finish, tears filled his eyes and emotion clogged his throat.

"A girl," Luke said, leaning over so that they were huddled together on the bed. A family.

"A girl," Finn cooed. "Hello, Serena Ann."

With each passing moment, he grew a little bit stronger, became more and more aware of his surroundings. They were in a surgical room, but the hallway outside was silent like it was abandoned. He was in the middle of the room in a bed, the rest of his body covered with a white sheet. He didn't try to move his other limbs yet. Frannie was at his other side, standing back to allow them a private moment but when he made eye contact, she burst into tears.

"I'm an aunt!" she wailed. Daryl was beside her, putting a gruff, comforting arm around her shoulders.

"I'm a grandpa," he said with pride.

Sorell, Pippen, and Conner were there at his feet, all smiling. Finn smiled back, happy that his entire pack family was here and...Felix? He remembered Felix's pivotal role.

"Hey, bro," Felix said cautiously. "Everything looks good from this end. Your staples are holding, but it is really important that you rest for the next two weeks, minimum. Pain management will be most important. I can order some narcotics. I have a pal in the pharmacy. But..." he just stopped talking, like he'd reached the end of the number of words he understood and was now trespassing on very confusing verbal territory. He shook his head. "You know what, love is love, if there is one thing I have learned working in the worst parts of the world is that love finds a way."

Was he blushing? Finn thought it had to have been the dwindling anesthetic that made him think Felix had glanced back to his pack.

Felix left quickly after that, saying that he needed to contact that friend to get the narcotics quickly but that he would come back to clean up all trace of them in the room. He left them with enough painkiller, gauze and wrap to keep the wound clean to last for the ride home and said to call if there were any changes.

Outside the clinic, Finn clutched the baby to his front, sitting in a wheelchair, trying not to hiss his discomfort every time they rolled over something bumpy. Luke hovered as it was, his arms outstretched, his hands open to catch or block. He moved to the side abruptly, obviously blocking Finn's sight from something that lay huddled on the ground. It was furry and very dead.

"Lucian?" Finn said.

"I forgot to tell you. He was here. I'm sorry, Finn, it had to be done."

"I understand. Do all shifters revert to their wolf form?"

Luke nodded grimly.

"There is still so much about shifters that I don't know. How will I be able to help raise our baby?"

"I'll teach you," Luke said, kissing both baby and father on the cheek.

EPILOGUE

Four weeks later and Luke wondered if he had really ever appreciated the amount of sleep he had been able to get before the baby. He also wondered what the hell he'd done with all those hours in his day. But he wouldn't trade a thousand sleep-filled nights for any moment that he'd had with his mate and child. It was coming on 5 a.m., and Luke could tell from the change in the baby's breathing that she was about to wake up with that special wailing alarm tone she'd spent the weeks perfecting. He hugged Finn to his chest, intent on enjoying the last few moments in bed with him. Finn's naked form wrapped around his body like the sexiest fucking blanket he'd ever had. Warm too. And satisfied. Every non-baby moment had been filled with loving his mate, proving to him every moment of each day that he was as wanted as the first time he'd seen him bent over in the kitchen.

Right on cue, little Serena Ann opened her mouth and wailed.

Finn mumbled against Luke's chest, "I'll get her."

"No, you rest."

Luke tucked his mate back in, warm and cozy as he pulled on a pair of sweats and padded over to the crib. Serena Ann looked up at him with wise eyes. "Hey, you."

Luke had the baby changed and was feeding her the first bottle of the day when Finn emerged, his bedhead stuck out in every direction, his own sweats sat tantalizingly low on his hips. The tiny line at his abdomen healed more and more each day. He sat down next to them on the couch, looking at them both with an expression so full of love it still threatened to choke Luke.

Luke's inner animal stirred, sensing something coming, something unusual.

"What is it?" Finn asked, seeing his changed expression.

Luke didn't answer. Instead he calmly passed Serena Ann to Finn. She never stopped suckling from the bottle. Luke stood, stepping to the door. Finn followed but remained far enough back so that he could keep the baby safe. There was a knock, light and quick. Luke wondered if Lucian's pack had finally come back for vengeance, not that they were owed any, but when Luke didn't take claim over their pack master's death, he was sure the last few weeks had been full of chaos. And maybe now they were beginning to prioritize. Luke growled.

He opened the door, and his jaw dropped. On the front stoop, the sun just starting to rise in the twilight sky behind him, stood Christian. His jacket was unzipped revealing a large, pregnant belly.

"Christian?" Finn asked, his voice high.

Christian looked exhausted and practically fell into their house. Luke caught him. He carried him to the couch and laid him down on the cushions.

Christian's eyes fluttered open. "Hey," he said breathily. "Do you mind if I stay a while?" His eyes shut as he passed out.

Keep reading for a sneak peek at the next book, Claiming Christian

THANK YOU!

Thanks to **you** for reading my debut novel, Finding Finn. I have one specific friend I need to thank, you know who you are. You set me on this journey and I am forever grateful! Thank you also to my lovely cover artist who is always open to my late-night emails and "quick suggestions."

About Me

Kiki Burrelli lives in the Pacific Northwest with the bears and raccoons. She dreams of owning a pack of goats that she can cuddle and dress in form-fitting sweaters. Kiki loves writing and reading and is always chasing that next character that will make her insides shiver. Consider getting to know Kiki at her website, kikiburrelli.net, on Facebook (www.facebook.com/kburrelli), in her Facebook fan group (www.facebook.com/groups/kikisden) or send her an email: kikiburrelli@gmail.com

ALSO BY KIKI BURRELLI

The Wolf's Mate, The Den, Bear Brothers, Jeweled King's Curse, and Hybrid Heat series occur in the same world and characters do make appearances throughout. While each series can be read and enjoyed on its own, if you prefer reading connected series in chronological order, here you go!

kikiburrelli.net/reading-order/

Wolf's Mate Series

(Wolf/Lion Shifter Mpreg and MMF)

The Den Series

(Wolf/Coyote shifter Mpreg and MMMpreg)

Bear Brothers

(Bear/Hybrid Shifter Mpreg and MMMpreg)

The Jeweled King's Curse

(Dragon Shifter Mpreg)

Hybrid Heat

(Hybrid/Bear Shifter Mpreg and MMMpreg)

Akar Chronicles

(Alien Mpreg)

The Kif Warriors

(Alien Mpreg)

Welcome to Morningwood

(Multi-Shifter Omegaverse)

Omega Assassins Club

(Wolf Shifter Omegaverse)

Wolves of Walker County

(Wolf Shifter Mpreg)

Wolves of Royal Paynes

(Wolf Shifter Mpreg)

SNEAK PEEK: CLAIMING CHRISTIAN

CHAPTER ONE

Claiming Christian is available now on Amazon!

Christian McGannon ran down the darkening street. His lungs demanded more oxygen, but his throat already hurt from swallowing as much air as he could for too long of a time. He wished he could remove his sweater and hood but then whoever was following him would realize they weren't chasing who they thought they were. Then, it would all be for nothing. His screaming calves, his aching chest. His fear.

Christian swallowed that fear down deep into his gut. It would only slow him down. He knew he was being chased. Not that he'd dared to turn his head back to see anyone. But he could hear them whenever he slowed down. They probably hadn't realized how athletic he was when they started. He'd done a handful of marathons and competed in tennis on the academic level. Though that wouldn't matter when his muscles eventually gave way, and he biffed it on the unforgiving concrete.

For Finn. Just a little bit longer, for him. Finn was the entire reason he was here. His friend had run into a bit of trouble. Finn had needed a distraction and being the kind of guy he was, Christian hadn't thought twice about helping him. He'd put on his friend's clothes, to dupe the people chasing Finn. Now, it was hours later after Christian had first started this crazy chase and he could only hope Finn had made it to somewhere safe.

Up ahead was the turn that would take him down the narrow alley between the bakery and the dry cleaners. It led to his apartment complex where, if he could get through the doors without anyone slipping in, he would be home free. Christian urged his leg muscles forward. They screamed and flailed, but he sped up, turning down the alley, only to skid to a halt.

A chain-link fence blocked his path forward, lined with barbed wire all along the top. The city must have finally started making safer changes to the neighborhood. Too bad those changes had possibly just killed him.

He scanned the alley. There were no doors on either side of the buildings, only a dumpster and a pile of crates. Next to those sat a heaping pile of crumpled cardboard. Other than some other random trash there was nothing.

Christian turned around just as a pack of three sweaty, burly men entered the mouth of the alley. They wore similar clothes, generic bad guy: dark, stained jeans and dirty button-up shirts. They looked a little like bikers with longer hair and copious amounts of facial hair. Each was well-muscled, which made sense. No one who didn't have some athletic prowess would've been able to follow Christian for long.

"Finally ran yourself into a corner?" the closest man said between mouthfuls of air.

"I don't want any trouble," Christian said, breathing hard but not quite as hard as the other guys.

"Neither do we. We just want to take you back to our pack master," the man said.

Pack master? Christian knew his friend Finn had gotten involved in some weird stuff. Apparently, it was some sort of gang led by a pack master. He pushed the hood of his sweater down. "I don't want to go with you anywhere."

The bad guy to the right inclined his face a little upward like he was smelling something. He growled. Not a person version of a growl, but a real, menacing rumble from the very back of his throat. "This isn't him!" he snarled. "This isn't the mate."

"What are you talking about?" the first guy said. "We've been tracking his scent for miles."

"Smell for yourself!" the other man said.

And then, weirdly, the first guy did sniff at the air. He narrowed his eyes at Christian. "You little asshole. We've been chasing after you for miles!" He lunged forward and caught Christian around the middle in some football line-backer move. Christian fell on the alley floor, hard. The air knocked from his lungs, and his back hurt as he slammed against broken glass, and other sharp things sprinkled on the ground. The other guy's big hairy hands reached around his throat and squeezed. Christian flailed, kicking his feet, gasping out for help.

At once, the man disappeared, seemingly lifted from Christian. He scrambled to his feet searching for the small switchblade he should've pulled out when he first discov-ered he'd been cornered. Honestly, Christian wasn't used to people getting mad and staying mad at him. Up until the moment the burly man's hands had wrapped around his throat, he'd thought he would be able to talk himself out of anything.

Christian turned toward the action. A fourth person had appeared. Christian didn't know from where. The other guys would've prevented someone coming from the street, and they had been alone in the alley. The new person moved with a jerky gait toward the men who had chased after Christian, like he might fall over at any moment. But when he reached the other men, his movements were smooth, efficient. His blows landed like powerful rapid-fire strikes, dispatching them to nothing more than a trio of would-be assailants.

His savior spun around, hunched over and breathed hard. His hands still clenched into dangerous fists and he crouched like a wild animal ready to attack. In that heart-stopping moment, Christian was scared. No, he was terrified and knew with absolute certainty that if this man meant him harm, then harm he could do.

Yet, through his terror, Christian could still see that this man was gorgeous—utter masculinity carved across his angular face. He had the darkest brown eyes that bordered on black. His hair was a glossy espresso-brown color and matched his closely trimmed beard and mustache. But, mostly, it was his innate sensuality that Christian noticed as if his every movement exuded sexuality. Ridiculously, Christian was almost jealous of the unconscious men behind the dark stranger. At least they had been touched by him. Handled by him.

Christian took a jerky step backward. What the hell? Handled? He brandished his puny knife in front of him. It hadn't seemed puny at first. Now it was laughable that it might keep him safe from this muscular mystery man. "Don't come any closer," he said without any real oomph.

The other man sniffed the air and staggered toward him like he was possessed, or possibly drunk. "What is that smell?" he asked with a surprisingly gentle southern accent. Then, he growled, obscuring any possibility of using the word "gentle" to describe anything about him. He narrowed his black eyes. "Take that jacket off," he ordered.

"S-stay away from me!" Christian couldn't believe his luck. Now a sexy, drunk homeless man was trying to steal his jacket.

The man lunged forward so quickly Christian couldn't see the movement clearly. One moment the man was a few feet away and the next he was right on top of him, groaning in pain. Christian yelled and released the switchblade. It stuck into the stranger's body. His strong hands went to the knife handle and ripped it out of his body. Blood covered his hands and the knife blade.

"Oh shit," Christian whispered.

The other man looked up at him with a look of hurt betrayal. "You stabbed me? You can't stab me. You're *mine*."

Christian's pulse quickened, and his stomach did a funny flip at the man's words. Then, the man crumpled. Christian caught him under his armpits. Every glorious pound of him was now like dead weight. This close, Christian could smell alcohol on his breath and possibly his clothing. So he had been drunk. "Hey, buddy. You can't pass out. I know shit about this, but I know you can't pass out."

"Not...passed out," the guy said with effort.

"I'll get you to a hospital. What's your name? Do you have anyone I can call?"

The guy laughed, a short bark that contained no actual humor and ended in a pained cough. "No hospital, no one to call."

"Well...fuck."

As if to cement his sentiment, one of the unconscious men moaned and shifted.

"*Fuck!*" He hauled the man over his shoulder. He had terrified him, yes, but he had saved him too. And, if Christian was really honest, this stranger intrigued him. Oh, and he had stabbed him. It wasn't like he could just leave the man to bleed to death. Or if the jerks woke up, to be beaten and then bleed to death. He gathered all of the man's weight and gave thanks to his workout regimen. He'd never missed a leg day.

That didn't mean it was easy to carry the muscled body out of the alley and around the building, taking the side street that led to his apartment building. He had to keep from laughing, if he started, he would probably drop his cargo, but it was kinda funny to him how close he had been to his home. If only he hadn't tried to take a shortcut. Even as he thought it, something in his gut rebelled from changing any step that led him toward the handsome, drunk, injured, terrifying man.

At the entrance, he swiped his card and the door beeped open. The moment it shut and the automated lock reset, he felt an enormous relief. At least now they wouldn't get beat up, or worse. The man groaned then, and Christian remembered guiltily that only he was now in the clear.

"Hey, hey, buddy," Christian set the guy down on the elevator floor, propping him against the wall.

"Derrick," the man mumbled. "Derrick Antoine Robichaud, the Third, not buddy."

"Great, Derrick. Happy to meet you. I'm sorry I accidentally stabbed you. My neighbor is a...well, not a doctor of people. But...I mean if you are sure you don't want to go to a hospital? Or even a free clinic? Well, no a free clinic would have to contact the police for a stab wound. But, then, it isn't a mystery who stabbed you. Though really, you stabbed yourself."

"You talk a lot," Derrick said, but not really in a mean way.

"I've heard that," Christian replied. That and just about every variation of, except Finn. Finn had never resented or been annoyed by Christian for never knowing when to stop talking. The elevator doors dinged open. Christian lifted Derrick back up, apologizing as the other guy groaned in pain. He managed to get his door opened and then settled Derrick on his couch before rushing out and pounding on his neighbor's door, praying he would be home.

Dr. Steven Phillips opened his door a crack, most likely having first peeked through his peephole and seeing Christian. "No, I do not have any more cookies—is that blood?" The middle-aged doctor's tone went from jokingly flirting to serious in a split second.

"Yes. It isn't mine. I stabbed someone. Accidentally." Did he have to keep emphasizing accidentally? Christian doubted it helped his cause. He was proven right when Dr. Phillips tried to shut his door on Christian.

"You should call the police then."

"I can't. Look, I know you aren't a real doctor."

"Excuse me?"

"I mean, a real person doctor. But he is literally bleeding to death on my couch right now. And who was it that went out and brought you your favorite turnovers from Susie's Bakery every day you were sick last year with the flu?"

"You," Steven said begrudgingly.

"And who pretended to be your boyfriend when you couldn't get that girl you met at the comic con to back off?"

"You got several free dinners out of that if I remember correctly."

"Oh, okay. I see how it is. Well, let's just call the comic con girl and explain the whole—"

"No, no. Let me grab my bag."

Christian nodded and waited, but kept his foot lodged in the door in case the doctor tried to pull a switcharoo on him. Honestly, he hated throwing the nice things he had done for his neighbor back in his face like they were debts that needed paid. Christian hadn't minded going to the bakery and during those dinners was the first time he'd had tapas.

Steven returned and followed Christian to his door. Christian put a hand on his arm, making Steven turn to him. "Before you go in," Christian said, the guilt already setting in. "You don't have to. I'm sorry about what I said."

Steven just rolled his eyes. "I know. Come on." He pushed open Christian's door and entered first. All of a sudden, he stopped and shrieked. "What the hell, Christian?" He stumbled back, running into Christian in his haste to get out of the apartment.

Christian's blood ran cold. Was the guy dead? He hadn't seemed that injured when he'd left him. He peered around Steven's fleeing form. There, on his couch was a huge, black wolf. No, huge wasn't the word to use. The wolf was ginormous. Christian let Steven run out of the apartment. He was already laughing like it was some hilarious joke Christian had pulled.

He went back in slowly. The wolf just sat on his couch and stared at him with wise, dark-colored eyes; they were almost black. He was well-trained for a wild animal. That was why Steven probably thought it was such a joke. Christian knew his eyes were wide as he approached, looking around for Derrick. Had the wolf eaten him? Where the hell did it come from? He didn't even think his windows were big enough for the thing to get through. The wolf jumped off the couch and somehow landed behind Christian, effectively cutting him off from his front door and exit. It took a few steps toward him. Its nose sniffed the ground.

"It's okay. Down, doggy," Christian whimpered.

At his words, the wolf's dark eyes looked at his face. Those eyes, so wild and untamed and yet, so familiar. He noticed a small amount of matting on the wolf's dark skin at his stomach, like blood mixed with fur. He felt like he was putting one plus one plus one plus one altogether. Finn and his new friends, the guys who seemed to be tracking him by scent, all of it added up to one very absurd conclusion.

Christian sat down on his floor. Technically, his legs collapsed from under him, finally giving out after so much exertion and stress—but, he didn't fight it. The huge wolf came trotting up to him, all dark fur and dark eyes.

"Are you...are you, Derrick?" Christian asked the wolf, feeling like a fool.

The great beast ran from him, into Christian's bathroom. It bowed its head over Christian's toilet and then vomited. It was the strangest thing for Christian to watch. His mom had a cat once that had learned how to go to the bathroom in a toilet. A huge wolf getting sick in his bathroom was no less odd-looking than that had been. And that cat had been entirely just a cat. Should he offer to hold back his fur?

"Can I get you anything?" There was no reply, but Christian figured he always wanted some cold water after being sick, so he ran into the kitchen and grabbed a cup. Then he remembered who he was getting water for and grabbed a bowl instead, filling it with ice and water from his fridge. When he turned to return to the bathroom, he stopped short.

Standing in his living room, gloriously naked, was Derrick. He had a body that would feature in Christian's every fantasy. Usually, Christian despised body hair, but on Derrick, the dusting of hair across his chest looked natural and added to his masculinity. His fingers twitched, fighting the urge to reach out and pet him.

"Is that for me?" Derrick asked, looking at the bowl of water Christian carried.

"Uh, well, it was for...you?"

Derrick smirked. He had a dimple when he smiled on his right cheek. Christian wondered what it would taste like. Maybe he needed to pour the ice water over his head instead.

"Do you have any Band-Aids?" Derrick asked loudly. Christian must have been staring. It didn't seem like it had been the first time Derrick had asked.

Christian set the bowl down. A little of the water sloshed over the side and onto his table. "I only have small ones. Oh jeez, I forgot about your injury. I brought my friend over to take a look but, you...he thought I was joking."

"Your *friend*?" Derrick asked, his lips curled up in a small snarl.

Christian thought he should be more offended than he was. "My neighbor. He's a...veterinarian. So, not quite the doctor you didn't want to see." He bent forward to examine Derrick's wound, and while he was bent over, with his head close to the man's navel, he remembered he was still absolutely naked. Christian blushed and stepped back hastily. "I'm sorry. It looks excellent. Your wound I mean. Not quite as good as just not having one, but it looks better than it did."

"I heal quickly."

"That's good because I don't think I can get Steven to come back. Plus, he'll want to know where the wolf went and...." Christian waved his hand in a circular motion in the air.

"You don't sound very surprised. Deal with this sort of thing often?"

He most certainly did not. Up until a few weeks ago, his life was predictably boring. He'd known where he would be, who he would be with and to an extent, what would happen. That was until Finn came back from his break and Christian had decided to take a leap and try to get to know him. Look how that had ended.

"I guess I shouldn't be shocked. You were wearing that shifter's jacket. You still kind of smell like him, but not as much. You should change your clothes. So you don't attract the wrong sort of attention again." Derrick bent down to grab his jeans and slid them up to his hips.

"I don't think Finn is like you."

"Who is Finn? Another *friend*?"

Christian lifted his chin stubbornly. "Yes. He is."

"Wow. He must be. That's the rudest you've been to me. If I don't count...." He indicated his knife wound that was impossibly smaller already.

"You should still get that checked out. I hear it isn't the surface injury you need to worry about but the bits and pieces inside."

Derrick shook his head. "Nah. If it were going to kill me, I'd know by now." He neared Christian, putting a hand on his shoulder and guiding him backward. Christian allowed himself to be escorted. "I assume this is your bedroom?" Derrick must have seen something funny in Christian's expression because he chuckled. When he spoke again, his southern accent was thicker, cajoling. "How about you go and change out of those clothes and find me something to wear while we wash mine. Between you and me they smell like garbage and cheap whiskey."

Christian thought they should smell like dog, but kept that to himself. Before he knew it, he had handed Derrick a pair of sweats and a cotton t-shirt, shut the door and stripped. Only when Christian stood naked in his bedroom did he stop to wonder why he was simply doing what Derrick had told him to.

He heard loud voices coming from his living room. Quickly pulling on a pair of basketball shorts, Christian hurried out to the angry voices.

Derrick had just slammed Christian's door shut and turned around, his eyes taking in Christian's shirtless form, but otherwise unbothered.

"What happened?" Christian asked, worry packed into each word.

"Nothing? Oh, that? Your neighbor came back. I sent him away."

"Why were you yelling?"

"Do you always do him favors?"

"What? I don't know, sometimes."

Derrick scowled.

"Why are you looking at me like that?" Christian backed away, suddenly very aware of his shirtless state.

"You're too nice," he muttered, coming close.

"There is no such thing."

Derrick had firmly inserted himself into Christian's personal bubble. He looked at him with a challenging glare. "Do you like me this close? Don't you wish I would back off?"

No. "Y-yes."

He leaned closer, his face inches from his. His dark eyes kept Christian prisoner while baiting him, demanding he stand up for himself. "Make me then. Force me out."

Could Christian force this man to do anything? He felt like a solid wall of heat. Derrick looked unmovable. More than that, Christian wanted to lean forward more than he wanted to push back. As if he could hear Christian's thoughts, Derrick's face came closer. His lips neared Christian's.

Christian's frontal lobe finally kicked in, reminding him of every reason why this was a bad idea. *You don't even know this guy. He turns into a wolf. He was mean to your neighbor. He just threw up.* Christian lifted his hands and firmly placed them on Derrick's chest, ignoring the rigid muscles, he pushed as hard as he could. Derrick stepped back and then stumbled. He bent over in pain.

"I'm sorry!" Christian said, going to help him, but Derrick waved him back.

"No, no, just my *stab wound* is all."

Christian had forgotten about it. Again. It wasn't his fault. Derrick seemed so fit, sturdy and unwounded it was hard to remember.

"I should probably take a nap anyway. I can feel a hangover approaching. Unless you have some whiskey in here that I can chase it away with?"

Christian shook his head, but Derrick had already turned from him, making his way back to Christian's couch. He lay down and shut his eyes, leaving Christian standing near his front door, dumbfounded. He looked around his apartment as if searching for someone to tell him exactly what had just happened. The day had started so normally.

Christian shrugged. It wasn't like he was going to kick a possibly homeless man out. And it was dark out. Of course, he had questions about the wolf thing, but that could wait until morning. Everything always made more sense in the morning.

Want to see how Christian is claimed? Claiming Christian is available today!

Made in the USA
Coppell, TX
31 January 2023